SEVENTH STAR

Volume 1

Written by: Jonathan Solis
Illustrations by: Tony Guisado

Novel Horizons 2021

ISBN: 978-1-955391-07-8 (Paperback)
ISBN: 978-1-955391-08-5 (Hardcover)

Written by: Jonathan Solis
Illustrations by: Tony Guisado
Edited by: Stephanie Diaz

Novel Horizons
www.NovelHorizons.com

Table of Contents

CHAPTER 1

First Day

Daedalus Notos couldn't believe he was finally here, on the day of try-outs. The sun shined brightly over the grand, grassy field; a brisk breeze wafting through the air caused the trees to sway gently and the grass to dance playfully. The time of great tranquility had arrived, and to greet it, a large assembly of men and woman, including Daedalus, stood at attention in front of a large stage, as if they were waiting for a concert to begin.

Daedalus glanced at all the heads around him, his hands itching with anticipation for try-outs to begin. This was his one and only chance to earn a spot at the prestigious Regulus University, a chance he'd been waiting for all his life and one that was supposed to start twenty minutes ago.

Just as he was beginning to wonder whether they'd all gotten the time or date wrong, the distinct clack of heels reached his ears. In the distance, he saw a beautiful woman slowly making her way toward the group from the road beside the field. She had an authoritative gait, but the lack of interest on her face made Daedalus think she didn't really want to be here.

As soon as she stepped onto the stage, she started yelling. "Hello, maggots, and welcome to your first day in hell! My name is Frederika Espada, and I have been given the *grand* punishment of being the overseeing 'educator' for you waffle-munchers! As such, you will address me as ma'am, Miss Espada, Madam Espada, or Instructor Espada. If you address me in any other way, prepare to deal with dire consequences."

Upon reaching the center of the large stage, she stopped and looked down upon the scores of students before her. She wore a black two-piece suit with aviator glasses, and her long, enticing lavender hair swayed in the wind, carrying an undeniable air of authority and dominance. Her posture and demeanor clearly communicated that if anyone wasn't afraid of her, they should be. Daedalus stared at her with bated breath, his heart thumping in his chest.

"For any one of you pea-brained, paper-skinned wastes of spaces who find what I say offensive," she continued, "I would like to direct you to that spot over there. It's called the exit. You may go there to console

your pitiful feelings any time you wish. But be warned that once you go there, you will not be allowed to return. Because Regulus has no space for tiny, whiny babies."

Frederika paced across the full length of the stage, staring down every single student she passed as the loud clack of her heels echoed across the field. Not a single soul dared to make a sound.

"With that out of the way, let's get down to business. You trash-in-human-skins are here because you want a shot at enrolling at Regulus University, which is quite possibly one of the finest establishments in the world. For reasons beyond my understanding, you louses have the *audacity* to believe you are worthy of joining the ranks of this wonderful school, and for the next three months, we will see if you've got the chops or if you are all a bunch of nots."

She stopped her pacing and turned on her heel, looking down at a male student who seemed to be leaning somewhat into the stage, holding his head at an odd angle. *What is he doing?* wondered Daedalus.

"You've definitely got balls for trying to look up my skirt," Frederika said with a snort. "I commend you for seeing an opportunity and taking it, but for your sake, I sure do hope you are much more impressive in other fields than you are in your 'secret' lecherous actions."

Frederika leaned forward, causing her black skirt, which only reached about halfway up her thigh, to rise up dangerously high as she put a leg forward to lean on it, exposing a portion of her black underwear. Daedalus's eyes grew wide enough to burst from his head.

"Bunch of no-good men like you have no chance at getting a woman, let alone a peek at what's inside their clothes," she spat, wickedly. "You lot would probably take any opportunity presented to you. None of you even have the balls to take the chance I'm giving you. How utterly pathetic."

Her voice was alluring and sexy, but undoubtably dangerous and lethal. Her tone inviting but her eyes threatening. Everyone, including Daedalus, swiftly turned their heads away from her, he and the other men among the group sweating from Frederika's obviously targeted glare.

"All right. Can't say I didn't give you a chance," she said, as she straightened and fixed her skirt. "As I was saying, you all have three months to impress me and to convince me that I should let you stay at this prestigious academy. Within those three months, if you give me the slightest reason to believe you aren't worthy, I will run you out of these fine halls without a moment's pause. No questions, no readmission. If you at any point feel stressed by this, overwhelmed, or need someone to talk to, once again, allow me to remind you that there is a special zone just for that. Right over there." She jabbed a finger in the direction of the road leading away from the field and the university.

Within the crowd, located in the middle near the back, an eighteen-year-old Daedalus looked around to see if anyone was already going to give up, but it seemed the harsh words of the instructor hadn't been strong enough to cause anyone to quit. At least not yet.

He certainly wasn't quitting. After years of hard work and taking on numerous odd jobs, he had finally managed to scrape together enough money to pay the application submission fee for Regulus. The university of his dreams and the place he needed to get into at all costs in order to become one of the strongest Radiants in the world. Which was his goal, at least for now, until he found something greater worth striving for.

As he looked around, though, seeing a myriad of colors wrapping around everyone—the aura of their abilities, and some of them sure had an exceptional amount—he knew it was going to be an extremely tough endeavor. One that he wasn't entirely sure he could overcome, but he would fight to prove himself, nonetheless, until he couldn't anymore.

"With all that out of the way, does anyone have any questions?" asked Frederika.

A few people raised their hands.

"Put your goddamn hands down."

Frederika scanned the crowd again, seemingly displeased and even disgusted by most of the students she was looking at. She even went as far as bringing her sunglasses down, revealing her beautiful amethyst eyes, to make especially bothered faces at certain students. Yet, despite that, she didn't say another word; she strutted off the stage and left all the students there confused, angry, and in some cases, terrified.

"What the hell kind of orientation was that?"

"I didn't pay all that money to come here to be treated like this."

"Who the hell does she think she is? I want to report her to the school."

Multiple students in the crowd started complaining once Frederika had left their line of sight, seemingly emboldened now that she was no longer staring them in the face. A sharp clack silenced all of them again as Frederika appeared to the left of everyone. One of the students right in front of her fell over clutching his chest, as if having a heart attack.

"You bunch of ingrates decided to complain once I was gone?" She glared at all of them in turn. "Talk about being beneath a worm. If you're going to complain, have the bravery to do it to my face or shut up! The next time

I hear a complaint behind my back, that student is getting sent home. If someone wants to submit an official complaint, the 'special' zone is right there." She pointed once again at the exit. "In short, for those of you who don't understand, because I can see this group is slow on the uptake, shut your traps and be grateful you were even allowed on the grounds!"

Frederika's booming voice echoed down the whole field before she lifted an arm and snapped her fingers. Daedalus kept his head down, not wanting to draw her attention to him.

"Now get the hell out of my sight, you mangy mutts, and head over to Training Dome Three for your skills assessments, ability tests, and mock battle! This will be the most important thing you do today, so don't screw it up. How you perform in this battle will determine your initial worth as a potential Radiant. And for those of you who don't know where Training Dome Three is, figure it out! You have thirty minutes to get there, and if you are late…kiss your worthless butts goodbye!"

* * *

"Damn it, damn it, damn it!"

Daedalus sprinted at full speed across the school grounds. He'd just been informed that he had gone to

Training Dome Four, and not three. Forcing him to use his Luvis to speed himself up as much as possible so that he could make the thirty-minute deadline.

Who puts two buildings that are numerically neighbors on opposite sides of the same campus!?

The dirt under his feet hopped into the air with each enhanced step he took. Next to him, despite him putting in his all to make it to the dome, countless other students flew past him. Luckily, he managed to crash through the front door of the building just as an energy barrier roared to life, completely blocking the entrance.

A series of thuds reached his ears as people outside ran into the unbreakable barrier. Groans and yells followed, as the former students realized they had just lost out on being able to enter the school for the rest of their lives. Daedalus winced on their behalf, but he didn't have time to feel sorry for others when he didn't even know if crossing the barrier meant he was in the green.

"Well, well, well."

A slow clap and a familiar clack of heels echoed down the hall that led deeper into the sports arena-like dome.

"Looks like you just barely made it by the skin of your teeth." Frederika gave him a wicked smile. "Although, I do have some bad news."

"What?" asked Daedalus, gulping in fear.

"You'll have to be paired with someone who doesn't have a partner. You see, we let people choose their pairings, but in this case, almost everyone else has paired up already. You are the lone straggler without a sparring buddy."

"And that's bad because…?"

"I'll show you."

Frederika motioned with her head, and Daedalus jogged forward to get behind her as she navigated through the winding halls of the training dome. He'd read all about the university, and knew this building was used for practice and doubled as a venue to host Radiant battles. Which was why it had countless areas empty for stalls, and thousands upon thousands of seats whose rows seemed to extend into the sky itself.

Eventually, the two reached the ground floor. Frederika pointed toward the far end of the dome battlefield, where a single person could be seen leaning casually against the wall. A young woman, around eighteen.

She was wearing form-fitting jeans, a white turtleneck tank top, and a black jacket with gold details tied around her waist. Her eyes held a bored, almost disinterested glaze over them as she watched the other applicants fight in the combat zones.

"No one has had the balls to partner with her," said Frederika in an oddly solemn voice.

Daedalus could have asked why, but he could clearly see why anyone would be afraid to approach the woman waiting there. Towering high over her person was a monstrous amount of Luvis energy that even from a distance struck a deep terror into his heart. It was also obvious to him that she was doing her best to hold back her aura. Which made her that much more frightening, because Daedalus couldn't fathom what her full power was like.

"She's really strong, isn't she?"

"You can tell from this far away?" Frederika raised her eyebrow at him, impressed. "Not bad. Yes. She has enormous potential. Although, because of that, trying to get near her seems to cause people to pass out."

"How do you live normal life like that?"

"You don't."

A short pause followed in the conversation before Frederika pulled a lollipop out of her pocket and popped it into her mouth.

"All that aside, she is going to be your partner. If you can actually get close to her, I'll give you some credit. Frankly speaking, with how weak your Luvis is, I'm already surprised you are able to stand near her at this distance."

"Does her aura only affect Radiants?"

"Normal humans don't have the capacity to sense Luvis. It's weaker Radiants' senses being overwhelmed that causes the terror-inducing effect."

"I see."

"Anyone unfortunate enough to get her as a partner is sure to be given the worst possible start for admission in Regulus history. Without a doubt." Frederika popped the lollipop out of her mouth. "It's like pitting an ant against a lion… It's suicide. But, unfortunately, she is an applicant and she needs a partner. Which, in this case, is you."

"Because I'm the last one."

"Correct. You catch on quick. I like that. Shame, though, that you won't get a chance to strut your stuff. Maybe in the next phase you won't be so unlucky, although you'll have to find a way to make up for your bad start."

Daedalus sighed and took a step forward.

Frederika grabbed his shoulder. "You're just going? Just like that? You aren't going to beg, ask for a switch, or something else?"

"I don't beg or complain. This was the hand I was dealt, and it's my fault I didn't get here faster. So…yeah."

Frederika brought her sunglasses down with her free hand and gave Daedalus a twice-over before letting him go with a shrug.

"Good to see some of the male applicants still have a spine. All right. If you wanted a drop of my respect, you've earned it."

"I feel so honored," Daedalus said flatly.

"As you should."

He redirected his attention to the woman in the distance, and the pressure against his body intensified with each step he took. By the time he was only halfway to her, the force pushing against him felt like someone was incessantly punching him in the chest and throat at the same time.

Is…is getting stronger?

Daedalus looked at the woman again and realized that her eyes were on him. He gritted his teeth as he stared back at her, trying not to lose his breath. After a few seconds, she turned her attention forward again. The extra pressure on his body vanished in an instance. He couldn't believe that just her gaze had that sort of effect. A chill went down his spine that urged him to give up, but he ignored it.

Finally reaching the young woman, Daedalus steeled his resolve and managed to make it right in front of her. "I'm here to be your sparring partner."

Her eyebrows rose in surprise that someone was standing next to her. She shifted her posture so that she was standing normally, no longer leaning against the wall.

"Okay. What's your name?"

"Daedalus."

"I'm Freya."

Freya stood at an impressive six feet tall, while sporting a well-proportioned and endowed Amazonian body that spoke volumes of how she wasn't just gifted in Luvis but also must've trained extremely hard. Every part of her seemed capable of inflicting tremendous damage, and that was without taking into account the effects of using her Luvis.

Her steel-blue eyes pierced deeply into Daedalus as she studied him through her glasses. She seemed generally unimpressed by him and his comparatively short five-foot seven height, yet at the same time, he sensed he'd gained a bit of her respect for managing to succeed where countless others had failed by accomplishing the simple task of standing in front of her.

"So…" he started.

Freya didn't speak another word, and instead made her way to one of the training circles. Her aura spooked the other applicants and made many of them pause their ongoing mock battles as she made her way past them with Daedalus following close behind her.

The whole ground floor of the dome measured roughly four hundred feet in diameter, which was small when compared to other venues like the Grand Regulus Arena, but was big enough for the purposes of hosting multiple mock battles. Since new Radiants hardly had the skills necessary to make use of big spaces, dividing the space into multiple smaller circles allowed whole groups of applicants to engage in their mock battles at the same time without running the risk of interfering with each other.

Although, real arenas didn't have a dusty, beige floor; they had diverse biomes that could be changed on a whim, ranging from forests to open plains to recreations of cityscapes that allowed Radiants to fight in all sort of environments. This both upped the challenge of battle and kept things exciting for audiences as they watched how their favorite Radiants adapted to different surroundings.

"Good job," said Freya as Daedalus caught up to her.

"Hm?" he said.

"Hm...congratulations?"

She seemed to be having trouble trying to express what she wanted to say, and Daedalus was having just as much trouble trying to decipher what her intent was. A problem that stemmed from how she spoke without any emotion in her voice.

"Are you…praising me for being able to walk beside you?" he asked.

"Yes…but I didn't want to sound condescending."

Daedalus could tell that she was being sincere and wanted to take the compliment, but while Freya thought he had overcome her powerful presence, in reality, he was just barely keeping himself in control. Ever since he'd started talking to her, Daedalus's body had been trying to react violently to every movement she made, be it moving her lips, shifting her eyes, or taking a step.

It's like I'm walking next to death… It's unbelievable how oppressive her aura is.

There was no doubt in his mind that Freya was an incredibly powerful individual, but what puzzled him was why she wasn't suppressing her aura more. That was what the stronger Radiants in the world did so that they could live normal lives, so why didn't she?

Is she…incapable? Is that why she's coming here? To learn how to be able to bottle away this power so she can finally live a normal life? Why hasn't anyone taught her before now?

"Are you ready?" she asked, pausing in her step and turning to face him.

"Huh? Y-yeah. Sorry. I was just thinking."

"If you're too scared to face me, it's okay."

"Fear is not a reason not to do things," countered Daedalus. "Fear is just a sign that you worry about your ability to overcome what is coming. I'll overcome that worry and prove I can stand firm where others couldn't."

"Admirable," she said. "Can you fight, though?"

"I'll sure as hell try my best. Fear or not, I'm looking forward to this."

She stared at him, unblinking. "You're...looking forward to it?"

"Of course." He shrugged and smiled. "Facing off against such a wonderfully powerful opponent right out the gates? What Radiant wouldn't be excited to see how they measure up against such an amazing person?"

* * *

Amazing? Wonderful?

Freya repeated the words this strange young man had said in her head a few times. No one had ever called her those two words before. More often than not, they used terms like "monster" or "beast." Some of the more dramatic people she'd met even called her the envoy of death. Not that any of those names bothered her anymore. But these new words were definitely throwing her for a loop.

"Frankly, I don't know if I can win," said Daedalus. "But I'll try my best. I'm always looking to challenge myself so that I can improve myself more every day. Someone like you just makes it easier for me, since I probably won't have to find a new 'ruler' anytime soon. Although, in the end, I'll make sure to surpass you too."

"You plan on using me as a tool to measure yourself against?" she asked. "And you plan to surpass me?"

"Yup. Do you think that's rude?" Daedalus gave Freya a wide grin as he chuckled.

A strange wave of relaxation rode through her body, and her eyes widened slightly and came to life. But she quickly recovered and kept her expression monotone.

"No…not at all."

"Great. Then show me what you've got."

Freya nodded, and the two entered the centermost area of the makeshift fifty-diameter ring. The moment they did, a small pinging sound came from a module that popped out of the ground right outside of the circle.

"Luvis energy detected… Combatants recognized," said an automated female voice. "Deploying barrier. Match beginning in three…two…one…"

CHAPTER 2

Tiger vs. Tiger

The moment the loud horn blared to signal the start of the match, Daedalus dropped into a tiger-like crouch so that he could begin his assault immediately. When Freya did little more than take her hands out of her pocket, he frowned, feeling a bit insulted.

"Don't blame me if you lose immediately!"

Daedalus let out his Luvis and dashed forward, but no sooner had he taken a few steps than the aura around Freya intensified, paralyzing him. His body, specifically his muscles, seized up and he couldn't move an inch. It was like they were forcing him to stay frozen out of a sense of self preservation.

I've already dealt with this before!

He gritted his teeth and, with a loud yell, forced his body to start moving forward again. Overcoming his instincts' built-in survival mechanisms as he overrode them through sheer force of will.

"Is that all you've got?" he called.

Freya tilted her head slightly as she watched Daedalus make his way forward at a respectable speed. Behind her emotionless exterior, he thought he saw a hint of curiosity in her eyes. As if he'd surprised her once again.

"No."

The pressure emanating from Freya intensified, and Daedalus paused as her aura gained a golden hue before exploding upward like a sparkling, majestic tower of energy. At the same time, he noticed that her hair and eyes started changing color to match her aura.

This time, though, despite it being obvious that Freya was unleashing more of her full strength, it did nothing to Daedalus. He had already forcefully shut down all of his body's innate responses to such stimuli, meaning that everything she was doing was effectively useless.

* * *

Freya's eyes widened in shock as Daedalus's fist made contact with her left cheek. *How is he doing this?* she wondered. But she quickly shrugged off the punch.

"You're the first person to be able to touch me in a long time," she said casually.

"I'm glad."

Freya took in the moment and cherished it. The day that someone managed to get close enough to hit her and at the same time, not feel fear toward her. The young man in front of her now was smiling defiantly as he held her gaze, and that made her feel excited in a way she hadn't experienced before. It was exhilarating.

At the same time, Freya's unleashed strength forced the end of most if not all of the matches still in progress, as the applicants looked upon her with terrified gazes. It took only a few more seconds for the whole battleground to empty. Everyone had fled to the outer area. Only Frederika remained, observing the duo with her arms crossed and an amused look in her eyes.

Daedalus, now free to move, started unleashing a series of punches against Freya with rapid intensity as he used the full extent of his skills in the "Striking Tiger Palm" fighting form. From his fist to his heels, he went at her with the ferocity and movements of a proud tiger, but they had little effect on Freya, who blocked each blow with the back of her hand.

"How can you so easily overcome pure terror?" she asked.

"Nothing easy about it. I'm just more scared of giving up than I am of your power."

A rouge punch raced at Freya, who found the rhythm strange but blocked it regardless. She found her leg knocked out from under her and in a powerful grip that began tugging on her to flip her toward the ground.

The sudden shift in tactic caught Freya off guard, but as she flew through the air, she twisted firmly and forced Daedalus's grip to slip before putting her own arms around him. Effectively putting him in a chokehold before she had even landed on the ground.

"Damn it!"

Daedalus struggled against Freya's grip, but despite his best efforts, he couldn't make her arms budge in the slightest. It was like solid metal had been put in place to hold him. In fact, metal probably would've been easier to break out of.

The fighting stagnated after that, as Daedalus continued to struggle against her hold to no avail. It didn't help that Freya was significantly taller than him, because that left him dangling in the air once she stood up straight.

"Oh, man. The world is darkening around me," he said, gasping. "I see Gram-Gram."

"Surrender then."

"Never!"

"You sure are stubborn."

"Never!" Daedalus cried, as he kicked his legs back. It didn't do any good.

"All right, all right. That's enough."

Frederika stepped in between the two of them and pulled Daedalus away from Freya by the top of his head. As she dangled him in the air, she patted Freya on the shoulder and gave her a curt nod. Then she put Daedalus on the floor gently before dusting her hands off.

"Well done," was all she said before walking off.

The two applicants were left looking at each other awkwardly, until Frederika appeared high in the air inside of the commentator's box. Her loud voice boomed throughout the dome.

"That concludes today's mock examination. Frankly, I'm extremely disappointed by how absolutely horrific the majority of you were. But luckily, the handful of you who are not absolute letdowns more than make up for that. The next step moving forward will be the assignment of your temporary dorms, which you will share with another person who…will probably be the person you were paired with today. They will be your roommate for the next three months before the final Orientation Tournament, which will be your final chance to prove to us if you are worthy!"

"Madam Espada, are you sure?" whispered a voice that was barely caught by the intercom.

"Yes, I'm sure."

"But didn't President Alice—"

"I know what she said, but that's too much work. Just make it happen. We already have all the duos logged. Just transfer the document over an—" Frederika cleared her throat, as if remembering she was still speaking over the intercom. "Anyways, tomorrow morning I expect you all to be here at exactly six to receive your new lodging. Now get out of my sight!"

Frederika stepped out of the box, vanishing from sight. Freya nodded to Daedalus and started leaving the large field, but paused when Frederika's voice returned as she seemingly ran back to say one last thing.

"Oh, and if you do anything that gives us a reason to kick you out in the meantime, or if we decide that your current standing at any time before the tournament is too low to recover from, we will kick you out. Cheers!"

This time, Frederika actually left the box.

* * *

Daedalus let out a long sigh as he thought about the next three months. If he had read the university manual correctly, every applicant had three months to gather points through different methods—some were supposedly kept a secret—which would culminate in their final score pre-tournament. Most people didn't seem to worry much about the three months, but he had heard that it could be perilous if not handled correctly.

Regardless, it was commonly agreed by all students that the biggest influence on whether you made it into Regulus or not was how well you did in the Orientation Tournament.

He walked up to Freya, who was putting her jacket back on. "Hey, so…I'm going to go talk to Instructor Espada."

"Why?"

"So, we can try and rearrange our rooms. It'll probably be awkward for you to live with a guy for three months, right? Maybe I can find another pair in a similar situation."

Freya fixed her jacket with a series of firm pulls before adjusting her cuffs and looking back at Daedalus. "I don't mind."

"What? Really?"

"Yes."

She fixed her hair and adjusted her glasses before heading toward the exit, her footsteps making a soft crunching sound. After a few steps, she stopped and looked back at Daedalus. He was still trying to process how easily she'd accepted living with him for three months.

"I'm hungry," she said. "Let's get lunch."

"Uh. Yeah. Sure, since we are going to be living together. Would be good to get to know each other a bite before tomorrow. Um. I look forward to being your roommate."

"Likewise."

Daedalus jogged to catch up to the woman he had just met, and she gave him a small nod as they started walking out of the building together. The intense aura circulating around Freya became almost inconsequential as Daedalus focused more on holding a conversation with her, and he ultimately stopped noticing the powerful energy that swirled around him, tinging everything in a majestic gold.

CHAPTER 3

The Old, The New, The Jarring

Time started passing quickly once the students all received their dorm room assignments, and just like Frederika had said, everyone ended up being put with their partner from the mock battle. A fact that created problems for some and enjoyable situations for others. Neither of which really applied to Daedalus, as he quickly realized that living with Freya wasn't as awkward as he'd thought it would be.

It turned out the two were a naturally good fit to room together. Their habits melded well and their personalities had a high degree of compatibility. In spite of that, certain things did cause problems from time to time.

"Daedalus, I'm done with the bathroom."

It had taken the better part of a week to completely move into the new dorm. Which had to do more with its big size than the amount of their belongings, since they both were fairly minimalistic when it came to decorations. Not that it mattered, since the space they now inhabited could easily be classified as a luxury apartment. It boasted two large bedrooms, a spacious living room, a wonderful kitchen, and a sizeable bathroom.

What made the bathroom special, though, was that, aside from the normal fixings, it was upgraded with two faucets, a jacuzzi bathtub, and even a single-person sauna space. Although the sauna space could fit two people if they squeezed in a bit.

"Freya...I'm as big an advocate of body positivity as any other person, but for the sake of my sanity, I really want you to consider wearing something more than just underwear when you walk out of the bathroom."

"I have a towel too," corrected Freya, as she held up the white towel draped over her shoulders that was barely covering her chest.

She had emerged from the steamy bathroom with only a pair of black underwear, a towel, and her glasses. Creating a sight to behold, as her whole body was put on private display for Daedalus to see.

On one hand, it allowed him to confirm that she was just as physically fit as he had assumed, with a body that matched her absurd Luvis power. On the other, that

very same kind of body being so "unclothed" in front of him created all sort of problems for him.

"You don't have to listen. It's just my two-cents. I'm sure I'll get used to it…hopefully."

"Used to what?"

"Do you realize how attractive you are?"

Freya tilted her head in confusion, and looked down at herself. She furrowed her brow. "Am I?"

"I feel like I'm being pranked. There's no way you don't realize how good looking you are. Even if we forget about all of that, and those"—he gestured vaguely at her chest area—"and the dump truck you've got going on, just your face alone would be enough to seduce probably any man and quite a few women."

"Dump…truck?"

"It means your butt is big."

Once again, Freya seemed confused by what Daedalus was saying, as she glanced at her own butt. "Huh. I suppose it's because I like doing squats. Is that a bad thing?"

"No, it's not a bad thing. It's just something guys tend to like."

"And why should I care about that?"

Daedalus started to open his mouth but put up a finger and stopped himself. She'd made a valid point. In this case, he was the one being unreasonable. People had the freedom to go about how they wanted in public and in their private life. If someone wanted to walk around naked, that was their right. How people reacted to it wasn't their problem, nor did they have a responsibility to care. The responsibility fell on the other party.

"I think I just learned something new."

"Does this make you uncomfortable?"

"I think the better question is, are you comfortable like that?"

"Yes."

"Then, it's okay."

"I see." She twisted her mouth. "I'm sorry if I don't understand a few things that 'normal' people do. I... My exposure to other people has been extremely limited. Most of my life I've just lived alone. I think you're the first person to really stay in close proximity to me for such a long time."

"'Cause of your aura?"

"Yeah."

Freya's aura was still as oppressive and as large as ever, but thankfully all the dorms in the university had walls that blocked this sort of energy from oozing out and affecting other tenants or the outside world. Making it so that Freya's "terror-inducing effects" were contained to the space she lived in.

Interestingly enough, the longer he stayed in it, the more Daedalus realized how little it was affecting him. At first, at the mock battle, it was like staring death in the eye. But even when they had gone to lunch, it seemed like he was quickly growing accustomed to being inside the "area of effect." Now, about a week later, he didn't notice it anymore unless it was pointed out. Even more peculiar, though, even if he did notice it again, it no longer made him feel scared.

"So, you've lived your whole life like that? Why didn't anyone ever teach you how to contain it?"

"They did. I've even tried learning how to do it on my own…but despite all that, I can only bring it down to this level. No one knows why, and every instructor eventually just gave up trying to figure it out. According to them, it was only a problem for the weak."

"So, they never bothered to consider how it would affect the life of a growing child? Her relationships, her chances of living a normal life?"

"Nope."

Bunch of lazy, no-good clowns, thought Daedalus.

"Well. How about I try and help?"

"Can you?" A drop of hopeful emotion leaked into Freya's voice.

"As you know, I'm not the strongest Radiant, but I'd like to believe I have a knack for Luvis manipulation and concentration...sorta. Here, watch this. It'll probably be easier to show you. It's not really useful for fighting, but it could have its uses."

Daedalus repositioned himself so he was standing in an open area of the living room. With a deep breath, he expanded his Luvis outward, creating the illusion that his aura was more powerful and vast than it really was.

Freya's eyebrows rose. "I didn't realize you were so powerful."

"I'm not! That's the thing. What I'm doing is, I'm expanding my energy so thinly that it takes up more space, but in a way that it's still dense enough that a Radiant will sense it like a normal, large aura."

"Interesting."

He pulled his aura back in until it returned to normal. "Logically speaking, if I can make my aura seem bigger than it really is, I should be able to teach you how to do the opposite. I doubt this skill is unique, though, so it might be better to just ask around at Regulus so we can find an instructor who knows it. I wouldn't want to teach you incorrectly or something. Regardless, I feel confident your problem can be solved. Even if it is a bit late."

Freya shook her head and walked into her bedroom. A few moments later, she emerged wearing a large baggy

T-shirt, and in her hands was a cute tiger plushy with a small top hat and monocle.

"Even if the university might have an expert, I'd rather take the help of someone I know who can help... So, I'd like you to help me," she said as she took a seat on the couch.

"And the stuffed animal?"

"His name is Mr. Tora. He helps me feel safe."

"I see. Hello there, Mr. Tora. A pleasure to make your acquaintance."

"Gao! Nice to meet you to!" said Freya in a deeper, rougher voice, as she picked up the plushy to cover her face. "Let's get to learning! I have great hope that you can help Frey-Frey with her problem! Gao!"

"I'll do my best," said Daedalus with a chuckle, taking a seat across from them. "So...first you want to meditate..."

* * *

A few days later, the new applicants finally got their temporary school IDs, which gave them temporary access to all the facilities located on the school grounds, while also marking the official start of their pre-admission classes. These classes were designed to measure the applicant's general knowledge and intelligence rather than actually teach a subject.

With IDs in hand, both Daedalus and Freya had the same idea of what to do first now that they had unlimited access to the school.

"Time to head to the gym!" said Daedalus with a grin. Freya nodded in agreement.

Both of them were eager to restart their training, so with a pep in their step, they got ready to head to the state-of-the-art Regulus gym complex. This meant donning proper attire, which in Daedalus's case consisted of sneakers, shorts, and a body-tight, white workout T-shirt. Freya chose to also wear sneakers but decided to wear spats shorts and a sports bra only.

But then, as they were leaving, Daedalus was reminded of a certain problem they hadn't faced in several days. No sooner did Freya leave the dorm than someone fell victim to her intense aura. Daedalus looked down the hall to see a prospective student tensed up like a pole.

"Uh…"

He wanted to say something to the poor guy, but after another moment, a shiver went down the student's spine before he fell back onto the floor with an almost comical level of stiffness. Completely unconscious, but fortunately, still breathing.

Well. That's not good.

Despite the duo investing all of their free time in Luvis manipulation concentration, little progress had been made in actually fixing the problem with Freya's aura. Which wasn't surprising, since it had only been a few days. In those few short days, though, Daedalus, with the help of his unique vision, had been able to figure out that Freya's problem might be rooted in not just how much Luvis she exuded but how potent it was.

In traditional Radiant teachings, the concept of hiding your own power revolved around being able to limit the flow of your Luvis. Technically, it was impossible to completely stop any Luvis from coming out of a Radiant's body, but to lower it to the point that it was undetectable was a fairly easy thing to do. Which is where Freya's problem came in.

Contrary to what she thought, Freya wasn't failing at lowering her Luvis flow; in fact, it seemed to Daedalus that she had brought it down to an even lower level then most Radiants should be capable of doing. Yet the same aura persisted, and the reason became obvious once Daedalus focused harder on what exactly her aura was made of.

Her Luvis density is a tenth of what a normal Radiant's is when they "turn off" their aura...but not even that is enough because of Freya's Luvis potency. One unit of her Luvis has to be at least equal to one hundred units of another Radiant's...

Daedalus knew that Radiants were born with different talents in Capacity, which was how big a Radiant's "container" for Luvis was; Potency, how strong a single measurable unit of Luvis from a Radiant was; and Regeneration, which was a Radiant's ability to "recharge" Luvis. Yet, he had never seen, heard, or read of someone who broke the known scale to the degree Freya did.

"Is something wrong?" asked Freya, noticing that he'd stopped walking in the hallway.

"Uh, I think we just knocked out that guy over there." Daedalus pointed at him. "Maybe we should wait until night."

Freya turned around, and Daedalus could see a sharp pain immediately overcome her eyes. All the joy that was there moments ago had evaporated instantly, and she calmly walked back into the dorm before facing Daedalus again. Which also made the fallen student flail back to confused life.

"Just go without me," she said.

"Without you? Nah."

"It's okay."

"Maybe to you, but how can I pass up learning the secrets of exercise from such a powerful Radiant? Besides, working out is more fun in pairs." Daedalus smiled.

"It'll just cause you more trouble. Not everyone is so weird that they can adapt to living inside my aura."

"Oh, I'm weird now?"

"Yes."

Freya looked away and made a subtle pouting face, showing Daedalus the most emotion on her face that he had ever seen. It motivated him to further push the topic of not going without her.

"Oh, well. I guess that's your problem then."

"How?"

"Because now you have to deal with a *weird* workout partner."

Daedalus walked back into the dorm and closed the door behind him before taking a seat on the couch and turning on the TV.

"I heard a really good movie just came out. Let's watch that to kill the time."

"Okay."

"And then, to the gym! Woo!"

* * *

"My existence has been reduced to pudding. I am a dessert now…but simultaneously a being made of constant pain. I have achieved balance…nirvana."

A moment of nonsense washed over Daedalus as he lay face first on the ground. His arms reduced to little more than jelly and his face burning hot, he waited for death's embrace to whisk him away to a better place without suffering. A place far away from this gym.

Off to his side, Freya had mild amusement in her eyes as she stepped over him so that she could head to the next station. Daedalus weakly crawled over the floor to try and keep up with her.

"You can rest," she told him.

"Rest…is for the weak! I can rest when I die!" declared Daedalus with a dramatic flourish.

"You might if you don't take a break."

"Ffffine."

Daedalus stopped a few feet away from the squat rack, and his head smacked back into the ground as his body went limp again. Returning to what he called his "pudding state."

In the meantime, Freya started setting up her bar and placing forty-five-pound weights on each side, one after another, until they reached a total weight of 360 pounds. As she did so, Daedalus managed to recover enough of his energy to pull himself up to a sitting bench.

"Is that your normal weight?" he asked, counting the plates.

"No, it's less."

Freya got under the squat bar and with seemingly little effort lifted it up and took a few steps.

"Uh...should I spot you?"

"It's okay. It's not that heavy."

With a deep breath, Freya's eyes sharpened and a raw intensity started roaring out of her. It felt like gusts of ethereal wind blowing over Daedalus, but rather than fear, he found it relaxing and cooling as the wind washed over him in continuous waves.

Just how strong is her body innately? he wondered.

For a non-enhanced Radiant, Freya was displaying constant feats of superhuman strength. It was one thing to do what she was doing while empowering herself with Luvis, but to do it without any power enhancement was simply mindboggling.

No wonder she's so powerful while using Luvis.

It was long ago established that Luvis made people stronger by multiplying their base strength, which was why it was extremely important for a Radiant to be physically fit. Workout, diet, routine—all three vital for reaching one's own max potential. Mental health was also important, since Luvis manipulation required a healthy mindscape as much as a strong body.

"She could probably throw me around without Luvis while I have my own enhancement on," murmured Daedalus with a chuckle, as he watched Freya do her set of textbook perfect squats. "It's pretty crazy."

Each muscle in her body moved with astonishing control. Every part of her body worked with the others in flawless harmony as she continued doing her squats. Even when fatigue started setting in halfway through her second set, with sweat drenching her body, her form remained immaculate. Only her slightly heavier breathing and the subtle fluctuations of her aura let Daedalus know that she was growing tired.

What a Radiant, he thought, grinning.

Daedalus had spent the majority of his life working to get into the best university for Radiants. He had driven himself ragged, broken bones, pushed his limits time and time again so that he could achieve his goals. He prided himself in believing that no one worked harder than him. But now that he'd met Freya, he was happy to see how wonderfully wrong he was.

"I'm done," said Freya, as she put the bar back and dismounted the weights. "Daedalus?"

"Oh, sorry. I was...just lost in thought."

Freya tilted her head, and Daedalus tossed a towel in her direction so that she could start drying herself off. She caught the towel and, in the same motion, cleanly kicked up a water bottle at her feet and snatched it out of the air before drinking from it.

"How do you feel about sparring a bit before we head back?" suggested Daedalus.

"If you want."

"I was thinking maybe you could help me with my forms, if that's all right."

Luvis proficiency aside, Daedalus thought back to when he had fought Freya and how she had reacted to his various attacks. In a different universe where she was at his Luvis level, he was certain she still would have won through raw skill alone. Which meant that there was a lot that he could learn from her, be it forms or even tactics.

She nodded. "Let's do it."

* * *

"Breathe. Focus. Strike."

Freya lifted her knee high into the air and, with a long exhale, stomped the ground before punching forward and sending a powerful pulse of raw force outwards.

"This is fairly different from the forms taught by the Great Families," noted Daedalus as he tried to mimic her motions.

The Seven Great Families were the founding families of the newer generation of Radiants, who not only possessed the raw power gained from Luvis but also possessed different abilities, some of which bordered on the supernatural. These seven families studied Luvis intensely and independently, and, over the years, had developed their own unique forms, which allowed them to manipulate Luvis energy in ways never before seen. The families had become powerful enough to rival the governments of the world.

"Because it is a form only know to my family," replied Freya. "Although, these are only the introductory forms, to help you control the flow of Luvis and give it proper form."

"But instead of generating fire or making lightning, it's simply enhancement?"

"Correct. Simple doesn't mean bad. To my family, it represents infinite potential to grow."

Daedalus repeated the motion slowly and tried to visualize his Luvis moving through his body in rhythm to his motions. It felt somewhat familiar but also new at the same time. He couldn't figure out why.

"You're pretty good," noted Freya as she gently adjusted his posture.

"I think it's because it feels a little like the form I use."

"Which is?"

"It's a form my mother used; it's called Striking Tiger Palm."

Daedalus did a slow, controlled roundhouse kick before shifting to his next standing position, where he took a deep breath and exhaled with the following punch.

"I thought your style looked familiar. Although, it seems modified."

"You've heard of it?"

There was long pause, and Daedalus's question died in the air, unanswered. He turned back toward Freya, his brow creasing.

"What's wrong?"

"Did the style she used look something like this?"

Freya whipped one leg around in a half circle that scratched over the floor until it was behind her. Then, she crouched down as low as she could like a tiger, with one hand acting as a balance and the other off a bit to the side with a claw hand. Taking a powerful leap forward, she whipped into a full horizonal flip using her whole body. It ended with a powerful roundhouse kick that created a gust of air. Kept in the air by the force, she then rapidly spun forward into a fearsome axe kick. The loud boom it made echoed throughout the sparring room.

"Whoa," said Daedalus.

Keeping her foot where it had hit the ground, she rotated on that same heel into a series of rapid kicks that looked like the strikes of a sinister whip. Her movements culminated into a tight, downward, rotating leap kick that would have easily obliterated the jaw of any opponent it encountered.

"That's…exactly what she used," said Daedalus, in awe.

"Then that is my family's fighting form."

He stared at her. "What?"

"I'm not sure how your mother learned it. We don't really openly teach it to others," said Freya, dusting off her clothes. "Although, I suppose it doesn't matter."

"I thought she created it, since I'd never seen it before."

"From what little I saw, I can see that yours is heavily modified, but it's the same base. If you're okay with it, I'd like to talk to your mother. See where she learned it."

"Oh." Daedalus's mood dropped. "Uh. I'd love to ask her too…but my mom died a long while ago. A freak accident of sorts."

"I see. I'm sorry."

"It's fine. I practiced this form using an old book of notes she had, which was how I learned it. I filled in the blanks using other similar forms as a reference. I guess that's why it became heavily modified. It's the only thing I really have that connects me to her, after all. That and a few other things she left behind for me."

Daedalus lifted his hand up to show off a red string bracelet around his wrist. It was simplistic, with only a series of obsidian pearls decorating it to denote a "top" for the accessory.

"Wards off bad energy. At least, that's what she told me…Anyways, I'm getting off topic. So, the forms?"

"Right. Striking Tiger Palm is probably different than what you learned, though. It harkens back to the basics of Luvis manipulation, and Luvis using this form is strictly for physical enhancement."

"So, no fancy tricks like shooting lasers or making explosions?"

Freya shook her head. "It relies mainly on skill and technique."

A gust of wind picked up, and Freya appeared behind Daedalus while still being in front of him. It wasn't until a second later that her afterimage flickered with a golden outline before disappearing.

Daedalus whistled, impressed. "That's fast."

"And lethal." Freya did a light neck chop to put an emphasis on her point.

It was true that the speed at which Freya could move seemed extremely oppressive, since not even his eyes could keep up with her motion. But he felt that there had to be something that more experienced Radiants had up their sleeve to deal with fast opponents. Otherwise, everyone would just focus on speed.

At the same time, he had to accept he barely knew anything about the benefits of Striking Tiger Palm. He had only learned it in bits and pieces from a notebook. He could hardly call himself an expert on the matter. Plus, it was that exact form that had led his mother to almost become one of the strongest Radiants in the world. So, there had to be something he was missing.

"If you want to master this form, you will need to push yourself harder then you ever have before," said Freya. "Even among my family, the ones who can truly grasp this technique are few and far between. Sometimes generations go by without creating a master. But the teachings remain due to the documents my families kept."

"Do you think I can master it?"

"I think you could."

"Also, a bit off topic, but how come you're talking a bit more than usual?"

"I enjoy this topic," Freya replied, her cheeks blushing red. "Leave me alone."

Daedalus started chuckling, and Freya gave him a firm but warm look before walking up to him and putting him back into his starting stance. Taking the hint, he refocused on the task at hand, and together, they went through the basic motions step by step.

CHAPTER 4

Grand Orientation Tournament

Daedalus and Freya quickly grew accustomed to life as roommates and as temporary Regulus Students. Every few days on a schedule, they would take long, boring tests, which unlike Daedalus, who did them with ease, Freya struggled greatly with.

Outside of the examination "classes" they took, the two spent most of their time training together or simply relaxing in the dorm. It was a tranquil time where more than anything else, the two simply got to know each other better and prepared for the upcoming Grand Orientation Tournament.

Following Daedalus's advice, Freya ended up realizing that by replicating his technique to spread out his aura, she could make her own Luvis thin enough that it became undetectable. Effectively eliminating a problem she had had for most of her life. The cost, though, was that if she lost too much focus, her aura would violently snap back and cause all manner of destruction.

To combat this, the two worked toward making the spreading effect a second-nature action. In the process, Freya accidently developed a secondary skill, a new ability that was an unexpected side effect of her spreading out her Luvis as far as it could go. Specifically, due to her own innate sensitivity to Luvis, even with her Luvis thinly spread out, she could still sense things that passed, touched, or affected it in any way. Giving her full awareness of all her surroundings in a several hundred-meter-wide space. Daedalus named this ability "Omniscient."

In that same timeframe, Daedalus gained a much higher mastery of Striking Tiger Palm, but unfortunately for him, that ended up being the full extent of his progress. Any attempt to replicate Omniscient, or other similar skills, ended in failure. Although his self-enhancement techniques did improve by leaps and bounds due to Freya's continued guidance.

Then, as quickly as everything had started, it began winding down to an end as the day of the tournament finally arrived. The final event that would determine who would be allowed full enrollment into the school and who would be left behind.

* * *

"Welcome, everyone, to the Orientation Grand Tournament! We are glad that everyone could join us today for this fun and exciting event that will wrap up Applicant Group B's trial period here at Regulus," called out a beautiful, melodic voice.

Standing on top of a podium that hovered high in the air, a petite, young-looking woman spun a long microphone stand in her hand as she talked. A warm smile lit up her face, and as she swung her microphone around, it became obvious that it was just a prop.

This air of cuteness that she gave off was augmented by her pink twin ponytails, her cute Lolita-style dress, and her porcelain-doll face that seemed impossibly flawless. All these traits together created a being of adorableness that was hard for the students and onlookers to ignore.

"I am proud to sanction this event for Regulus University under my name, Alice Alcyone, as the president of this wonderful school!" Alice spun her mic like a baton and slammed it into the floating ground connected to the podium. "Let us all give these brave participants our utmost and sincerest support as they undertake what may be one of the most important tournaments of their life, here in the Grand Regulus Arena!"

The Grand Regulus Arena, one of the three biggest battlegrounds for Radiants, was a venue whose prestige was unmatched and only equaled by one other arena. For multiple years, the GRA had hosted major tournaments for Radiants from around the world, including the Grand World Championship Tournament, the most important tournament in existence, where one hundred of the world's best Radiants battled it out to become one of the seven Pleiades. The champion of the tournament was crowned the Seven Star Ruler.

As expected of a world-class arena, the seats for the audience spanned every inch of the stadium, numbering well over 100,000, with the very top row holding skyboxes that were reserved for only the most important people in the Radiant world. Namely, high-ranking members of the Seven Great Families or the Pleiades themselves.

"Over one thousand meters of terrain are available for these student-prospects to battle in. As you all know, this arena can hold a wide variety of environments, but like usual for this tourney, we will be keeping the terrain as simple dirt."

Alice threw her hand over the arena and, as if on command, the tiles that made up the floor began glowing brightly before transforming into patches of dirt.

"Before we begin, I'd also like to give a warm welcome to an esteemed member of the Pleiades who has decided to join us today. I'd like to introduce everyone to the youngest Pleiades, rank four in the world, the Armament Queen, Madam!"

All the lights in the arena shifted to focus on one of the skyboxes. Sitting calmly inside it, with her legs crossed, was a beautiful woman with long pale blonde hair, wearing a light purple qipao.

"Hello, everyone!" she said brightly, waving at the audience. "I hope today's tournament is a good one. I have heard great things about the students in this batch, so I hope to be the first to witness the beginning of the new powerhouses in the Radiant world!"

Madam stood up and used both hands to wave as the crowd burst into cheers. Among the current Pleiades, Madam was undisputedly the most popular and well-loved. The reason why wasn't just because of her charming personality and beauty; it was also due to her being the most sociable among the Pleiades. While most of the others kept to themselves, rarely going out, she often hosted events and threw parties.

In spite of all her public appearances, though, no one knew much about her. Not even her real name was public knowledge. She was simply known as "Madam" or "The Armament Queen." There were numerous rumors as to why this was so, but none had enough concrete evidence to be believed as fact. In the end, people only knew two things about her: that she was the fourth most powerful Radiant in the world, and the she owned a majority of the bars and hotels in the country.

"I wish all of you good luck and urge you to try your best," she continued. "And no matter what the result, remember to never give up and to continue pursuing your dreams no matter what!"

Madam gave the crowd another smile as her voice echoed out beautifully, seemingly caressing everyone's ears with each word. She sat down as the lights returned to their normal positions, focusing back on Alice.

I wonder which one of these is Freya Stryker, thought Madam, her face becoming serious. Her eyes swept over the group of participants, seeking out the young woman she was looking for. *I've heard a lot of rumors regarding her. She might be worth getting to know.*

The appearance of family heads and Pleiades at events such as the Orientation Grand Tournament was seen as an extremely rare occurrence. Usually, they only appeared if one of their family members was involved, but in Madam's case, she'd made the trip solely because she had heard an extremely powerful new Radiant "brimming with potential" was participating.

She's a clever girl. She knows how to suppress her aura well. It's pointless in this environment, sure, but crucial in the real tournaments. Good that she's mastered it early.

While part of Madam was impressed by Freya's ability to mask herself, another part was somewhat irritated that a beginner student was capable of hiding herself from her. Even if it was ultimately inconsequential, because she would see her fight, the idea that she couldn't just see who she was looking for somewhat bothered her.

"Now then, everyone," called out President Alice, clapping her hands. "Let us begin!"

* * *

"Qualifier's round...number seven...Radiants, at the ready!"

"Well, this is absolutely not the best way to start this."

Daedalus took a long deep breath as his eyebrow twitched slightly. His body stood deathly still, and he started smacking his lips as the young woman in front of him gave him a friendly, albeit monotone-faced, wave.

Right off the bat, in his first match, Daedalus had been paired with the one person he was hoping not to face off with until at least the semi-finals—Freya. If he had gotten at least a few matches worth of time to show off his skills with different opponents first, things wouldn't be as bad. Going up against Freya first thing was just a stroke of bad luck.

It's one thing to like a challenge, but...come on, thought Daedalus, fighting back a groan.

Freya continued waving gently at him until the timer began counting down for the fight to begin. At that point, she took off her signature black jacket and tied it around her waist before entering her fighting stance.

Daedalus clenched his fists. *Let's get this over with.*

"Match starting...three...two...one..."

A sharp beep echoed throughout the arena as the crowd became deathly silent in anticipation for the next match. Everyone was waiting for someone to make a move with bated breath.

"Here I come, Freya!"

Daedalus launched himself forward, but after his first step, he felt the space around him growing heavier. A deeper, more radiant gold hue colored the landscape.

She's condensing her aura.

Freya's aura was released from its forced expansion, and its full strength was revealed. Gasps rose from the audience, and out of the corner of his eye, Daedalus noticed someone spill their drink from shock. Luckily for most of the audience, though, the barrier keeping them safe also acted as a Luvis containment field. Thus, only Radiants of sufficient power were capable of feeling what was going on inside the battlegrounds.

Against any other opponent, this shift in environment might have ended the battle immediately without a single blow being thrown. But after spending such a long time inside of the aura, helping Freya control it, such a change didn't matter to Daedalus. He didn't even need to force himself to continue moving; he moved as naturally as he always did, without hinderance.

The first blow connected with a ferocious burst of wind that kicked up dirt for many feet. Locked in a fierce battle of strength, Daedalus and Freya's fists clashed. Their continued struggle generated small shockwaves as they jockeyed for superiority.

A sudden shift in posture from Freya caused Daedalus to fall forward as their fists slid over each other. Primed to unleash a powerful knee, Freya locked Daedalus's arm. She let out a small noise as he flipped her over in response, using her own speed and momentum against her.

* * *

"How peculiar."

Madam fixed her posture to get a better look at the scene unfolding under her. She had been growing rather bored with the performances so far, until now. The aura she could sense from inside the containment field was oppressive and powerful enough to belong to a first-class Radiant. That much was true, which was impressive to see in a student. But what ended up catching her attention the most was the male Radiant, who was seemingly moving freely inside such a dense field of Luvis.

His Luvis is miniscule. He shouldn't be able to withstand that sort of pressure. Is he simply enduring it? It's obvious this girl is the one I was searching for, but what unexpected gem has she brought with her?

* * *

Freya tried to counter Daedalus like she'd done in their first mock fight, but she looked pleasantly surprised to find herself shoved back and upside down as soon as she tried to. This forced her to catch herself on the ground with her arm and one knee, as Daedalus kept his grip on her wrist to slam her downward.

Without wasting a moment, Daedalus flicked his leg out to try and land a powerful heel on Freya's chin. All he caught was air as Freya flipped backward before landing and immediately dipping deeply into her crouching tiger stance.

A short pause in the fight followed, as the two stared each other down.

The crowd had also started holding their breath as the fighting stopped. Most of the audience came to simply watch for fun, since tickets were almost free, with little expectations other than a casual day out. Not one of them had expected to see such a heated, high-skill, hand-to-hand battle.

Blow after blow, kick after kick, each fighter met the other in what seemed to be a deadly, yet almost rehearsed battle. Each reaction was nearly perfect and every counter seemed to read into the mind of the opponent. But Daedalus and Freya's battle wasn't something born of scripted combat; rather, it was the result of constantly training against each other. Day in and day out, they'd fought in the training halls, and now, it showed, as they had a sturdy grasp on each other's inner thoughts.

If she's doing this then... Daedalus thought.

...he's going to do that, Freya thought.

A flurry of punches was quickly countered by expert blocking, and a powerful kick was reversed. Until suddenly, Freya started speeding up significantly and the battle shifted in her favor. Her Luvis wrapped itself around her body to form a golden glow. The usual transformation of her hair and eyes then followed as they became majestically golden.

Normally, this change would signal the coming end to the fight, but Daedalus stood resolute in front of Freya as a majestic blue concentrated around his feet.

"Since when can you do that?" asked Freya, quite calmly.

"It's something I've been working on. Pretty cool, huh?"

He dashed forward with astonishing speed and began pressuring Freya. For a new student, Daedalus moved quickly and with intent. A trait that many "speedsters" lacked early on as they simply tried to abuse their quickness. Yet, not even this sudden burst in speed was enough to topple the mountain called Freya, as she quickly adjusted to his speed.

Each time his leg moved, it was to segue into another kick. All manner of different kicks were being merged together into a flowing chain of attacks. Despite Freya's effort to counter him, she found herself continuously pushed back by the other leg as he started fighting from what was effectively a handstand.

It was all in vain, though, as Freya increased her strength further and again went on the attack.

Daedalus quickly found himself losing ground, but he stood firm against the increased assault. Yet, things continued to look worse and worse until finally, he missed a crucial block, which resulted in a kick landing that snapped his head back.

Damn it!

His legs tried to give out from under him. The whole of all his muscles in his legs became non-functional as the force of the kick resonated through his body. It was taking all of his willpower just to stay conscious from the devastating singular blow. Thus, there wasn't much left to funnel to his legs, and like a cut marionette, he eventually crumpled onto the floor.

"Radiant down detected…countdown…three… two…"

Mustering up more of his strength, Daedalus managed to get back up onto his feet just before the automatic machine announced the match was over. On wobbling legs, while flexing his jaw, he brought his fists up to continue the fight. His eyes were dull, and blood dripped out of his mouth, but he wasn't ready to give up.

Once again, the two Radiants exploded into a flurry of blows, but this time the engagement ended almost too quickly, as Daedalus missed his footing. A devastating blow to the face left him on all fours. Still, he was determined to continue.

By now, even though Daedalus could put his guard up, he stumbled in place as he forced himself to stay standing. Through sheer force of will, his condition was still above what was considered okay for the automatic system monitoring the match.

A violent gale exploded outward as Freya vanished from sight.

Where did she go?! Daedalus thought as he rapidly looked from side to side.

In an instant, Freya appeared behind him and delivered a gentle, yet firm chop to the back of his neck. Immediately knocking him out in the best way she knew, and putting an end to the match. Daedalus didn't have time to process the blow; he simply fell to the ground with his guard still up.

"Radiant down detected…countdown…three…two …one! Match over!"

* * *

The crowd exploded into cheers, clapping wildly. The battle had exceeded well beyond the expectations of the people there, and even Madam gave the two a small clap before standing up to fix herself another drink.

On the ground, Freya picked Daedalus up gently and with a deep bitterness, she took him to the medics who were waiting just outside of the barrier's walls. Her anger wasn't directed at him, though; it was directed at herself and the unfortunate twist of fate that had pitted them against each other so soon. Most likely ruining his chances at being accepted into the university.

CHAPTER 5

A Brighter Tomorrow

"It's unusual of you to do something so...cruel," said Frederika, standing with folded arms and narrowed brows. "Matching those two against each other? Right out of the gate?"

"I needed to see how she would act," said Alice with a shrug. "It's good to see she can make the hard choices when needed. And not jeopardize herself. As for *him*, hopefully he'll use this to improve in the future."

"Does it matter if he does, though?"

"I'll give him a few more chances. Out of gratitude for Emilia."

"You're bending the rules out of gratitude?"

"I'd say it's being lenient more so than bending the rules. After all, he's shown great improvement! Plus, it isn't like I'm letting him into the school strictly because of that. He's simply getting a retry."

"I can't say I agree with that."

"It's a good thing you don't have to."

Alice smiled at Frederika as she finished adjusting her dress and, with a small skip, she picked up her microphone stand before making her way toward the podium to announce the winners.

For a majority of the tournament, she had simply rested and practiced singing on the large TV behind her. This wasn't because she didn't care about the event; she just didn't need to see it. From the sounds that echoed out of the arena, even as she sang and danced to her own music, a picture-perfect image of everything happening during each fight was visible to her in her mind. She used it to mentally grade every single student.

"Should I start with my left foot or right foot?" Alice wondered aloud as she alternated between feet.

"Does it really matter?"

"Oh, Rika, you really don't know anything about the art of performance, do you?"

"My job isn't to perform. Unless you mean *perform*," Frederika countered, while making a throat-slitting motion with her thumb.

"Well, that is a performance in and of itself. A different kind of art. Not the kind of thing we do here, though."

"Publicly."

"Hush, Rika. Anyways, I'm feeling rebellious, so I'll start with my left foot! Oh! I'm such a bad girl. Teehee! Non-dominant foot start for my walk? Gives me chills!"

"Yes, you're horrible…" Frederika sighed as she rolled her eyes.

Alice nodded her head, tapping the ground with her stand-cane. Immediately, all the lights in the arena turned toward the podium and Alice, as she stepped out into the open to the enthusiastic applause of the audience.

"Hello again, everyone! I'm so glad you all enjoyed the tournament!" Alice cheered, her voice echoing out harmoniously and easily covering the full arena. "It's now time for the results of the tournament to be announced, as well as the crowning of the Champion!"

The podium lifted off the ground as soon as Alice was standing on it, and made its way up toward the center of the arena with *blub blub blub* sounds that Alice had gotten custom installed into it. It was pointless, but she enjoyed it because it made her ascent and descent "cuter."

"It was a long, hard-fought tournament filled to the brim with talent! Many came, and only a select few will be allowed to stay on these prestigious grounds. And only one will have the honor of being called Champion. So, without further ado, let us all cheer for our new Champion, Freya Stryker!"

Alice clapped her hands rapidly before twirling her mic stand and pointing it at Freya, who was sitting patiently in the stands with Daedalus to her left. As the lights focused on her, she seemed conflicted about what to do, but after a few encouraging words from Daedalus, she stood up and made her way over to the secondary podium that flew down to her.

"An amazing performance with an astounding show of Luvis and martial arts ability," continued Alice. "Truly, a talent like this student is a rare one to come by! Everyone, let us cheer for her some more! Clap, clap, clap!"

* * *

The crowning ceremony began like usual, and Daedalus watched with genuine enthusiasm, loudly cheering for Freya. She blushed at how fervently he was yelling. Eventually, he somehow managed to get the whole audience to begin chanting, "Stryker," making Freya even more embarrassed, but notably happy as she gave everyone a small wave that was mainly directed at Daedalus.

This went on for a few more minutes until President Alice continued going over many different things about the school, the meaning of the tournament and other mundane things most people didn't care for. Then, the students all held their breaths at the same time as she summoned a projection with a list of names. Each name was in order from best performance to worst, omitting those who didn't make it into the school. All ranked by numerical order.

Each applicant had sweat beading on their forehead as they looked at the list. As certain students found their names, they'd finally resume breathing and slump over in immense relief. In contrast, students who didn't find their name once they reached the end of the list reacted in a variety of different ways. Some sat in depressed silence; others put their face in their hands and cried; some shouted in anger. Only a few took it in stride.

Of those few, one was Daedalus. When he didn't find his name on the list, he simply let out a long sigh as he tried to control his emotions. A deep pain sliced through his heart, and his eyes dampened briefly before he rubbed the liquid away.

I had a good run, I guess. I did what I could and it wasn't enough.

Daedalus rubbed the side of his head before beginning to think about what his next steps would be moving forward. If he couldn't get into Regulus, then that meant he would have to try other universities, although all the other schools of equal prestige to Regulus were outside of the country and not financially feasible for him to attend due to the relocation costs they would require.

"Oy. Notos."

Next to him, Frederika appeared in the chair that was previously occupied by Freya. She had her legs crossed and was twirling a lollipop between her fingers. She stuck it into her mouth.

"Instructor Espada?" said Daedalus, his brows scrunching in confusion.

"You can just call me Frederika."

"Uh. All right."

"More importantly, I saw your performance against Stryker. A valiant effort but ultimately hopeless. You still gave a good showing, though. Enough to impress me and the President. Unfortunately, the way the system is set up, the second you lost your first match, you were more or less doomed."

"I gathered as much."

"Which brings me to why I'm here. You see, we've decided that you have potential. Although, it hasn't been cultivated enough to warrant acceptance. So...here."

Frederika tossed a wooden stamp that had an intricate, solid gold head, and Daedalus watched it fall onto his lap. Confused as to what it was.

"That is the seal of Regulus. It's a very special and precious item, as I'm sure you have figured out by now. Whenever you fill out your application next year, use that to stamp the authentication space. It will allow you to apply as many times as you want."

"What? Why?"

"Like I said, you have potential. Unlike most of the worms that crawl around here, you're more like a grasshopper. But you need to be more than what you are now if you want to enter these venerated halls. Because of that, President Alice has decided to award you that."

A chill went down his spine as he carefully lifted up the seal. It had the renowned "Seal of the Roaring Lion" coat of arms on it. It was a very special seal, and to have the ability to put it on anything was an honor beyond what words could capture.

"If you abuse this seal, though…there will be *dire* consequences," finished Frederika. For emphasis, she crushed the lollipop between her teeth.

"Right…"

Frederika threw herself into a standing position and with a short two-finger wave, flickered out of existence with a gust of wind.

After she was gone, Daedalus continued handling the stamp. He involuntarily clutched it as a few tears flew off his face.

"Are you all right, Daedalus?"

Freya had finally been released from her podium and come back. She had a sad look on her face. Her eyes caught the subtle wet drops on the floor from his tears.

"Yeah. I'm just...you know. So proud of how well you did in the tournament," replied Daedalus, with a sniff and a big smile.

"I-I'm sorry you didn't make it... I—We can still...I'll make time...if you go to a nearby university..." She bit her lip hard, as if fighting back her own tears.

Daedalus could see her aura beginning to react violently with her emotions. He hadn't expected her to care so much about him not getting in, especially when she should be celebrating her own achievement. He supposed she didn't have any other friends, besides him.

"Hey, hey. It's all right, Freya," soothed Daedalus, patting her shoulder. "Today, I wasn't worthy, but you were. Tomorrow, maybe I will be!"

"Students can only apply once. What tomorrow?"

"You'll see." He winked at her. "I promise you that much. One day, I'll be back at Regulus, and I'll be a student here too. A real, full-fledged student. In the meantime, though, I want you to do me a favor."

"What?"

"I want you to try your best to become the greatest Radiant ever. I don't want you to slow down or lose sight of the prize because of someone like me. Or anything, for that matter. I want you to promise me that you'll do the best you can do. Every day. All week. All month and all year. I want you to be so *awesome* that when I see you again, I can be like, 'This is my friend! Look at her go! I'm this awesome gal's friend! Ye-ah-ya!'"

Freya let out a hard breath of air, almost like a chuckle. "That's weird."

"Yeah, but will you do it?" Daedalus wiggled his eyebrows at her.

"Of course."

"Great! Then, how about we grab some food?"

"Food?"

"Yeah! To celebrate how well you did. It'll be my treat! Anything you want."

"But…"

"I told you. It's fine. It seems my luck hasn't been bled dry yet. So, one day, I'll be back. That's my promise to you and I plan to keep it. For now, this is your time in the limelight. You're going to be the star today, so don't spare another thought on me."

"All right…but, when have you ever been lucky?"

"Hmm. Well, I think I got lucky getting to meet someone as awesome as you."

Daedalus stuck out his tongue, and Freya shook her head before gently shoving him.

"Weirdo."

Daedalus grabbed Freya by the hand and led her out toward the exit of the arena, through the tunnels. On their way out, several other students congratulated her, but it seemed there were a multitude of people who were dissuaded from coming near her due to Daedalus. Why this was the case, neither of them knew, but both of them noticed the strange behavior and didn't really care.

"I know this great place," said Daedalus. "It has the best sandwiches!"

"Mhm. Sandwiches."

"I had a feeling you'd be in the mood for one."

The two left the arena and headed down the grassy yard, continuing to make casual conversation. For Freya, this helped alleviate some of the guilt she was feeling, but for Daedalus, a part of him was still hurting and fearful. Yet, despite that, as he continued talking with Freya, as the tranquil winds blew and the bright sun shone beautifully over the landscape, a certain calmness eased into him. One that gave him a sense of peace and told him that everything was going to work out, somehow.

CHAPTER 6

Regulus University

TWO YEARS LATER

"That's a nice photo."

Daedalus put his hands in his back pocket as he looked at a framed picture inside of the Hall of Legends building at Regulus University. The photo, unlike the others that were filled with many people, held a singular person standing stoically for the camera in a beautifully crafted white qipao with gold detailing.

His attention shifted to the right of that photo, where another almost identical photo hung.

"Freya Stryker, 'Gold Prominence.' Two-time Amateur League Champion." He chuckled. "Isn't that wild?"

A deep fondness filled Daedalus's eyes as he looked at Freya in the photos. She looked almost exactly as he remembered her. Except that back then, she didn't have the fancy fighting outfit. He'd figured she'd get one eventually from the school for being a "superstar."

Ever since his first failed attempt to get into Regulus, Daedalus had spent as much time as humanly possible training. Living at home with his dad, he'd devoted himself to honing what he learned from Freya and refining his Luvis control for the entire year following the tournament.

Unfortunately, he once again failed to earn admittance to the university, despite doing better in the second tournament. But he didn't let that dissuade him and finally, on his third attempt, he managed to get accepted into the school after putting on an even more impressive display of his talent, utilizing a new technique he'd created.

Daedalus flexed his hands and continued examining the two photos. He wondered what might have changed over the years, like if Freya would remember him or if she had moved on to a different world that he wasn't a part of.

These thoughts floated around in his mind, but for some reason, Freya's golden eyes seemed to soothe him of his worries. It was as if both photos conveyed some sort of message telling him that she was waiting for him. Yet, that made little to no sense, because her face was as expressionless as it always was.

"If you ask nicely, I might be able to get you an autograph, if you're interested."

A confident, feminine voice came from behind Daedalus, and he spent one more moment admiring the two photos before turning around.

"That's okay. I was just catching up. I'm not rea—"

Daedalus froze mid-step as his eyes fell upon a familiar pair of glasses in front of a certain pair of beautiful brown eyes. A wave of emotion swept through his body, and he leaned forward with a hard laugh.

"What are you doing here?" he asked before standing up straight.

"I'm here to meet someone extremely important to me."

"Really? Who would that be?"

"It's a guy. You might know him. I met him a while ago, back when I first applied here."

"Really?" He frowned. "I thought I was the only one you talked to at the time. Well, I suppose I didn't really pry into your personal life. Still, it's unexpected."

"I'm talking about *you*."

"Oh."

Freya walked up to Daedalus with a confident stride that seemed more aloof than he remembered. In fact, her whole demeanor was much more refined, powerful and self-assured. As if she was no longer afraid of being herself.

"So, you really did it." she said.

"Yeah, I told you I would, didn't I? But look at you. Two-time champ. What an honor that you'd take time out of your day to speak to me." He did a mock bow before her.

"Stop it." Freya chuckled.

He grinned. "But really, you've done amazing. I'm happy for you. You also seem to have changed a bit over the last two years."

"Well, a certain someone had more influence on me than I thought."

"Who?"

"I'm still talking about you."

"Oh."

Freya shook her head, and a warm smile appeared on her face that Daedalus had never seen before. It really drove home for him how long it had been since he'd last seen Freya. It occurred to him that a lot more things might have changed then he had originally thought. Still, he was happy that Freya remembered him.

"What happened to your hair?" she asked.

"Oh, just...a side effect of all my training."

"You overused your Luvis, didn't you?"

"No...yeah," he admitted, scratching his head.

In an effort to make it into the school, Daedalus had pushed his body past its limit more times than he should have over the span of two years. Eventually, the stress began wearing out his body severely, which resulted in multiple problems that came and went if he neglected his rest. One of the only permanent effects, though, ended up being the new streaks of white that now ran through his hair.

"Just as crazy as I remember." Freya shook her head and smiled.

"By the way, have you heard about the riots happening in eastern Broadstand? A lot of non-Radiants are pushing for stricter laws. Saying we are out of line and whatnot."

"No, I haven't heard anything."

"Really? It's been all over the news. It's even started a few smaller protests across the world. I think it has to do with the death of a few civilians in a recent Radiant-related crime."

Freya stared at him with a blank expression, seemingly uninterested, but at the same time, her brow furrowed like she was really trying to remember something related to what he was saying. Eventually, she gave up and let out a small sigh.

"More importantly...I was wondering. Would you be interested in being my roommate again?"

"Yes."

"Well, that's a—wait. Did you just—"

"Yes."

Both times, Daedalus responded without hesitation.

"Oh. Well. Great."

Daedalus threw his arms up and gave Freya a hug. Her eyes went wide as he lifted her into the air, although her feet still brushed the floor despite the fact he arched his back to lift her higher.

"You missed me a lot, didn't you?" she asked.

"More than you think."

"Oh," said Freya, her cheeks blushing at his directness. "Well...I also...missed you quite a bit."

She swayed from side to side as Daedalus rocked his shoulders before finally being put down. A huge smile painted his lips, and his enthusiasm continued to be a source of obvious embarrassment for her until he brought his fist up.

"Bumpsies?"

"...Bumpsies."

The two bumped fists, creating a small spark of blue-gold energy where their fists collided. Their hands then "exploded" back as they wiggled their fingers, and more sparks flew before they both spun together into a hip bump.

"Has your butt gotten bigger?"

"Probably," replied Freya. "I've needed to buy new jeans a few times."

"Not a terrible problem to have, if I'm being honest."

"Maybe not for you but, it eats into my money. Plus, it makes me an easier target to hit."

Freya slapped her hip with a stern look on her face, and the two stared at each other. The air between them became oddly serious. Maintaining direct eye contact, Daedalus then slowly poked Freya's hip before bringing his hand back to his side.

"Damn straight it does."

The atmosphere grew more and more tense; the two looked like they were on the verge of breaking out into a fight. But then the mood shifted as Freya began chuckling and Daedalus broke out into a loud laugh.

"What are we even doing?"

"I don't know," replied Freya. "How about we head over to the dorms. Where's your stuff?"

"Still at home. Since the term doesn't start for me until a month from now. Although, since I'm moving in with you again, I can just call up the school movers and have them take my stuff to—"

"Dorm 4991."

"Wait, isn't that…"

"The same one from two years ago. I just stayed in it."

Freya shrugged her shoulders, and the two started making their way toward the dorm. As they walked, they caught up on everything that had happened over the two years they hadn't spoken. For Daedalus, his story was fairly simple, as it consisted entirely of training, but Freya had gone through a lot more. She weaved a tale of epic proportions about her climb to the championship title.

"So, no new relationships?" she asked, as the conversation between them slowed.

"No time. No new friends, still on that single life game… I'm also out of touch with my family…should honestly call Gram-Gram…but yeah. How about you?"

"Nope."

"Uh…no as in you won't tell me, or no as in there isn't anything new?"

"Nothing new. It's a personal choice… I learned the hard way that not everyone is as noble or as endearing as you."

"What happened?"

"Too many people tried getting *too* friendly with me and then too aggressive. It didn't end too well for them, though," finished Freya, flexing her fist.

"Ah. Well, I can see why...since, you know, you're super attractive and...a really famous Radiant. But it sucks you only got to meet crappy people."

"Not all of them were bad. There was this really nice guy I met early on. He helped me a lot, but then he just up and left one day. It was partially my fault...but I knew if I waited long enough, he'd come back. Still, I was very sad when he left, so I expect him to make it up to me."

"I didn't have a choice!" exclaimed Daedalus, throwing his arms up. "I know you're talking about me. You aren't even being that subtle about it anymore."

Freya snickered as Daedalus shook his head.

"How do you feel about going to get a drink?" he asked. "To celebrate our grand reunion."

"Hm. I have a thing about drinking alcohol around people, because there's usually no one I trust there."

His face fell again. "Oh."

"So, I guess it's good that you're going with me."

"You really like that gag, don't you?" he said, rolling his eyes.

"It's the only one I practiced for today. More importantly, there's a bar just off campus. I've heard it's fantastic. Good food too apparently. I've been waiting for someone to go with."

"Well, then I guess you're wait is over."

She smiled. "I guess it is."

* * *

"Another!"

Daedalus slammed his fist into the table as he held up his empty shot glass. Next to him, Freya munched on an order of extra spicy buffalo wings. Randomly, she stuck one into Daedalus's mouth. He munched on it while nodding his head approvingly.

"Another!" called out Freya, as the wings ran out.

The Burning Ox was a popular and old bar establishment located right outside the school grounds. It was rumored to have been built before Regulus existed and even before the rise of Radiants. The wooden building boasted beautiful hand-carved furniture with all manner of decorations that made it feel like they were in a different country altogether. It definitely lived up to its reputation of being a high-quality, long-established place of drink.

And like all old, well-known places, the establishment had a unique set of rules for its patrons, which included giving their orders "old yeller" style.

Customers had to yell out their orders to the staff going around, who would promptly fulfill them.

This made things a bit awkward for Freya at first, since she was normally the strong, silent type. But after a bit of encouragement, she joined in on the fun with Daedalus, who took to the rule naturally.

"You need to try these sliders, Freya."

"Here, try some loaded fries."

The two ordered different entrees and appetizers from the menu, making sure not to overlap, and they promptly shared with each other anything they deemed "worthy." This resulted in a fun little round-robin system with food and drinks.

As they enjoyed themselves, Daedalus noticed that a group of people sitting on the other side of the bar had been observing them for a while. They looked inconspicuous enough, but he knew Freya had also noticed them, because of how her Luvis was focusing near them.

"What do you think they want?" whispered Daedalus in between bites of his wing.

"To cause problems."

"Good thing I'm a pretty good problem solver."

"Are you? I thought you were a troublemaker."

Daedalus picked up a napkin, crumbled it up, and tossed it at Freya, who chuckled as it bounced off her forehead.

"At a bar, though? Does this happen on campus?"

"Occasionally. You'd think they'd give up by now."

Freya finished cleaning off a wing and dropped the bone on the plate they'd been using before cleaning her mouth with a napkin.

"I feel like I'm in one of those old school movies," said Daedalus. "You know? The cheesy ones where brawls just break out in the middle of restaurants, bars, or like…gas stations."

"Yeah…" Freya sighed.

"Why, though?"

"Some of the Great Families don't like a 'nobody' having the Amateur Champion title."

"Ah, politics…"

The table had four women and two men, but on closer inspection, Daedalus noticed that the neighboring table, which hosted another four women and four men, also seemed to have similar intentions in mind.

"Here they come."

One by one, the group at the table started standing up, but before they had taken a step, a hooded figure stepped into their path and rested an arm on the shoulder of the person who seemed to be the group's leader.

This newcomer was tall, easily six feet like Freya, with a seemingly sporty build. Daedalus couldn't tell for sure, considering they were wearing baggy pants and a very loose hoodie. Still, the person sat down with the leader and spoke to her. A look of fear crossed her eyes before she shoved away the hooded figure and stood back up.

"Don't give me that! Stay out of our business!" yelled the woman. "We don't get in the way of your family business, so stay out of ours!"

The hooded figure was thrown off the seat, but instead of falling, they threw one foot under the table, which hooked under it, and they remained suspended diagonally until putting their second foot down to return to standing at their full, intimidating height.

"Now, get out of our way," growled the woman.

"Who is that?" asked Daedalus, whose face was turned away from the scene by Freya.

"Someone who needs to mind their own business. Or else they'll get in more trouble."

Freya shook her head before standing up, and signaled for Daedalus to stay seated. She started making her way toward the group. Daedalus had never seen so many people tense up at the same time. The moment they noticed Freya making her way toward them, they all looked like deer staring into headlights.

"I told you to mind your own business, Electra," said Freya once she stood next to the hooded figure. "Did you think the hood was sneaky?"

"Perhaps, although, as a Lady of the Electra, I can't just openly partake in these sorts of things without some sort of disguise."

"A hood is a disguise?"

"I also have these on!"

The hooded figure threw off their hood to reveal a beautiful young woman's face with long, silver hair that shone like moonlight. On her face, though, was a pair of comically cheap-looking glasses with a fake nose on the bridge and eyebrows as part of the upper lens. Daedalus bit back a chuckle of laughter.

"You're stupid," said Freya.

The young woman shrugged. "I think it's pretty clever."

"If you wanted to be disguised, wouldn't it be better to hide your most noticeable feature?"

"My curves are hidden, though. And my chest? That's why I have the baggy clothes."

"I meant your hair."

She looked up and opened her mouth to reply, then looked back at Freya while wiggling her finger at her like she had made a good point. She then turned toward the group while continuing the motion until she finally put her hand down.

"I knew I forgot something."

This woman's voice, unlike Freya's, which was mature and cool, had what Daedalus could only describe as posh undertones with a certain formality to it. She sounded like a princess trying to sound like a commoner or, at best, a woman who was so full of herself that her voice couldn't help but sound condescending. Yet at the same time, it was oddly alluring and pleasing to hear.

"Prominence…"

The leader of the group tried to make herself known by growling out part of Freya's moniker, but it seemed that neither of the two women in front of her were interested in what she had to say. All she could do was let out an awkward growl.

"Listen, can we do this later?" asked Freya, with an audacious level of calmness.

"Only if you agree to forfeit the next championship," responded the group's leader. "It can be to Iris, here. Or any other member of the Great Families. But the next champion needs to be from the Seven."

"I personally wouldn't take the offer. Not very satisfying, winning without beating the strongest Radiant," said Iris, crossing her arms.

"You wouldn't understand," hissed the woman. "You're a disgrace to the Electra household. No one in your family likes you. You are only tolerated because of your strength, and even that is laughable because you can't even beat a nobody from a no-name family!"

"How harsh. Although, I suppose it's true."

Iris shrugged and took the insult astonishingly well, but around her, small sparks of electricity came to life, hinting at her subdued irritation at the woman's comments. Similarly, Daedalus noticed Freya's aura intensifying, showing her anger on Iris's behalf.

"On the other hand, why does commoner *trash* think they can talk to me like that?"

Iris's calmness melted away like a morning mist. A sinister, almost sadistic smile spread across her lips as she slammed her hands on the table. Electricity sparked to life around her, and her eyes gained a dangerous gleam that sent a shiver down Daedalus's spine.

"You should all really know your place. Groveling in the mud like worms suits you best. Instead, you band together like disgusting rats to try and take on something you can never overcome."

Her sharp words and condescending tone intensified, and Daedalus felt like he was watching another Frederika. Only, instead of Frederika's generally uncaring disposition, it seemed like Iris was genuinely going out of her way to verbally murder the people in front of her in a particularly cruel manner…and she was enjoying every second.

The group's leader snorted. "Don't get cocky just because you're the daughter of the Elec—"

A sharp slap resounded through the restaurant, and everyone fell silent. Iris's hand was floating in the air still in motion from delivering a firm hit to the cheek of the leader. The woman's face turned a deep shade of red as her temper exploded.

But before she could lunge forward, Iris grabbed her full face in her hand and sent a frighteningly strong current of electricity through her body. The woman didn't even get a chance to scream; all her muscles locked up and Iris tossed her onto the floor, rigid as a rock, before dusting off her hands.

"Disgusting."

"You didn't kill her, did you?" Freya casually poked the fallen woman with the toe of her shoe.

"No, she isn't worth the trouble. She'll be fine in a few minutes once the current discharges."

The woman looked awake, but with a glazed quality in her eyes. A sight that struck fear into the hearts of the other people in her group.

"W-we weren't hired to deal with an Electra," stuttered another woman. "T-this is beyond our contract."

"Then do please make your departure," said Iris. "Promptly."

The group of people looked at each other and ran off. Two of them picked up their fallen leader, and within moments, they were all gone with money left on the table to pay their bill. Daedalus couldn't help staring at Iris, impressed.

"There. Much easier than you planned, was it not?" Iris smiled at Freya. "Perhaps we should make a sport of this sort of thing. Seeing as they enjoy sending assailants after you so often."

"Why do you have a hoodie on you?" asked Freya.

"As a member of the Electra, the daughter of the head, no less, and the second best Radiant in the Amateur League, there are things you must prepare! For me, it is these sneaky clothes to keep the fans from swarming me. Not everyone can conveniently alter their appearance like you."

"How did you know they'd be here?"

"I didn't. I was doing my rounds, enjoying the simpler things in life, and I could feel their intention like a foul stench. Completely horrific. So, I came to sort things out...or at least try to, but that woman was exceptionally...dedicated...to her task."

"I see. Thanks."

"Of course! You may be my rival, but I'll be flipped like a pancake if I allow ill to befall you. What merit would there be to me winning the tournament knowing I could never surpass you?"

The two continued talking as they walked back to Freya's table. Daedalus was still glancing around to make sure no one else decided to try and launch a sneak attack. He figured it was unnecessary, though, considering that Freya had her Omniscient skill. At the same time, the patrons and staff who were watching slowly came back to life, and everything returned to normal.

"Who's this?" asked Iris, with her chin.

"A friend."

"I see. Quite a cute friend."

"Thanks," said Freya and Daedalus in unison.

Daedalus lifted an eyebrow at Freya, confused why she'd said that. She looked away with a tinge of pink on her cheeks.

"Daedalus Notos," he said, standing up with his hand out. "A pleasure to meet you."

Iris looked at Daedalus's hand for a second, then took it with a firm grip. "Iris Electra."

"Always interesting to meet a member of the Seven Greats."

"Interesting? Not an honor?" she asked, as she released his hand.

Daedalus shrugged. "No offense, not really all that into the worshipping cult aspect. I think it's cool, what they do is cool, and that some of the members are cool, but that's about it."

Freya slid into her seat across from him. She grabbed some wings and began eating again, seemingly paying Iris no more mind. Iris, on the other hand, had also moved on from Freya and was examining Daedalus with a neutral but still intense look in her enchanting yellow eyes.

"Hm. I'll allow you two to enjoy your meal in peacc. Enjoy the rest of your night, Stryker."

Iris put her hood back on after adjusting her hair. She left the bar without saying another word. Daedalus could see her Luvis whipping around her until she vanished in a burst of lightning right outside the entrance.

With the departure of both the would-be assailants and Iris, the two friends continued eating the night away in peace. Both chose to pretend the previous commotion hadn't happened. Hour passed filled with food and talk, until they decided to see who could handle the spiciest wings, creating a whole new endeavor to endure.

Eventually, the night drew itself to an end, and the bar made its final calls to start closing tabs. By then, Daedalus was having a hard time walking, but luckily for him, Freya easily tossed him over her shoulder and carried him back to the dorm.

CHAPTER 7

Measuring Up
to Greatness

The next morning, the sound of a TV playing the news roused Daedalus awake. As he shuffled on the couch, he vaguely remembered falling asleep at the bar and shot up straight to figure out where he'd ended up.

"Who, what, where, when, why?" he yelled.

"Me, carrying, at the bar, last night, because you drunk yourself asleep."

Freya's voice came from beside him. He turned his head to see her sitting calmly in her couch chair, watching the television with her legs crossed, while holding a cup of tea.

Like usual, Freya was in her comfortable home loungewear, which consisted of a pair of snug booty shorts and a crop top that barely covered her sizeable cleavage. Interestingly enough, rather than giving off sexy vibes as one would expect, she instead held the visage of a tranquil thinker, deep in thought. A mature, cool, and calm air hung over her as she continued watching the news.

"I was right," said Daedalus, rubbing his eyes.

"About?"

"Your hips have gotten wider."

Freya blinked a few times before putting down her teacup and turning toward Daedalus. She looked like she was trying to figure out what exactly had inspired him to make that comment. Then, in the same moment, she abandoned the investigation with a sigh.

"You seem really caught up on that. If you're that obsessed with it, we can just measure them."

To most people, Freya's suggestion would've seemed outrageous and out of the question, but Daedalus wasn't most people. In the past, during the three months they spent training together, he had actually helped her log a lot of her fitness information to track her progress. This included using a measuring tape to get the size of her bust, waist, and hips.

"Is the tape still in the same place?" he asked.

"Should be."

"You don't use it anymore?"

"It's too annoying to measure myself."

Daedalus walked over to a cabinet table located right under Freya's TV. Inside of the drawer, he rummaged through a few random things until he picked up a roll of white measuring tape.

"Do you still remember how to?" asked Freya, as she stood up and walked into an empty space where she could stand comfortably.

"Yup. So, your hips?"

"All three."

Freya lifted her arms up and rested them on top of her head as Daedalus whipped out the measuring tape and slung it with practiced ease around her. He then tightened it around her hips but let go of the tension a few times, much to Freya's confusion.

"Springy." He chuckled.

"Having fun?"

"A bit."

Freya rolled her eyes but let him continue doing what he was doing. As Daedalus finally stopped messing around and tried taking the actual measurement, she flicked her hips back.

"Oops."

Her butt rammed into Daedalus's face, and he fell over. But, because he was still holding on to the measuring tape, Freya was dragged down onto the floor with him, much to her surprise. She landed heavily on top of his stomach.

"Oof. There goes my air," wheezed Daedalus, his grip finally releasing the tape and instead gripping Freya's hips to try and throw her off.

"Still springy?" she asked, unbothered by his hands as she brought more of her weight down onto him.

Daedalus let out another deep wheeze as the little air left in him was squished out. "Very. But heavy."

He squeezed her butt, and Freya flicked his forehead, then casually stood up to return to her previous position. Daedalus took a bit longer to recover due to having to gulp air back into his lungs.

"I don't think I need to measure you're hips anymore…" He groaned as he used Freya to get back onto his knees. "I-I'll just move on…"

Daedalus straightened his back to wrap the tape around her waist. He then stood up after a few seconds to measure her chest, since her waist was exactly the same as he remembered, if not a bit thinner. This wasn't very surprising to him, since Freya seemed to always have a consistent balance of fat and muscle around her core.

"Interesting. Your chest is tighter than it was before."

"Probably because of all the upper-body focus I've been doing. Although, it's a shame they didn't get any smaller."

Freya brought her arms down as Daedalus removed the tape and walked over to grab an old notepad from inside the cabinet drawer. Nothing had been written on it for a long while, since he logged Freya's last measurements. He dutifully began filling out the updated information.

That was when Daedalus heard the jangle of keys, and he looked up to see a set flying toward him. In an instant, he swiped them out of the air and spun them on his pointer finger with a confused look on his face.

"Those are the dorm keys," Freya said, while looking at the clock. "I need to go to a photoshoot... Just make yourself at home and we can organize your stuff whenever it shows up."

"Photoshoot? Is that something you like doing?"

"Mandatory, although it pays well too."

"Must be rough being famous."

"Yeah..." She sighed.

Freya seemed extraordinarily unmotivated to go, but there really wasn't anything Daedalus could do about the commitments she had. Her reluctance made a lot of sense to him, since he knew just how much Freya liked keeping to herself and out of big group things. If there was something that Freya valued most, it was her privacy, which was why it was a huge honor and shock that she was so willing to allow him into her space.

"You want me to make some of my famous spicy ramen for when you get back?" suggested Daedalus.

Freya froze mid-step, her posture perking up. She turned slightly to give Daedalus a small nod. Then, with a bit more excitement in her step, she went to her room to get changed and pack the outfit she needed for the photoshoot.

Daedalus's famous spicy ramen wasn't a very special thing in and of itself, but after the first time he made it for Freya, it had become her all-time favorite dish to eat during their time together.

It was a simple thing to make, requiring a pack of instant ramen that Daedalus would cook with chicken broth instead of water. He also added chipotle sauce and finely diced white onion to the stock before putting in the noodles and finishing with a few leaves of cilantro as a garnish. This, when mixed with the spicy seasoning packet that came with the ramen, created an interesting and exciting flavor.

I only wish I could make it as good as Mom used to...

Freya called out from her room, "I'll be back in eight hours."

"All right, I'll have it ready by then."

After Freya left, Daedalus finally had time to think about his situation, and he realized that even though he was in the dorm, he had literally nothing with him. No clothes to change into, no toothbrush, no food. At least he had his wallet and cellphone.

I guess I'm walking home to pick up my stuff. I wasn't planning on moving into the dorms for a hot minute, but this works too. I just need to...

Daedalus slapped his forehead, remembering that he had completely forgotten to talk to the school coordinators about his move-in date. He let out a groan. Standing in line and organizing that was probably going to eat a bunch of time alone, but it was something he had to get done. That could wait until after he got clothes, though, since he didn't want to get caught wearing the same stuff two or even three days in a row.

* * *

Following the completion of what he needed to get done, Daedalus found himself with more time on his hands then he had expected. In fact, it had taken him no more than three hours to talk to the school and grab his things from home. So, rather than lounge around, Daedalus ended up heading to the gym to work up a sweat.

In his shorts and shirt, he entered the building and beelined it straight to the punching bags. The training area was marked by a red glowing outline as soon as he entered it. This line acted as a warning for other patrons so that they wouldn't wander too close and accidently get hit by someone in the middle of an intense practice.

Daedalus unlashed a ferocious flurry of palm strikes and wrist blows into the punching bag as he walked around it. He also used kicks where necessary, as he practiced his combos and tried out a few things he had been working on.

This continued for about an hour of non-stop practice until a familiar voice came from behind him.

"That's a familiar form."

Daedalus paused after unleashing one final roundhouse kick, and he turned on the ball of his foot. Standing in front of him, right outside the red line, was the silver-haired beauty from the night before. Unlike yesterday, she was wearing standard workout attire, which consisted of yoga pants and a baggy, sleeveless crop top that exposed her surprisingly well-defined abs as well as the sides of her sports bra.

"Oh, you're...Iris, right?"

"Correct."

Last time he had seen her, he couldn't get a good idea of her body type, but now he could tell that she was every bit as lethal a Radiant as Freya was. Even her Luvis aura seemed almost as ferocious. The biggest difference

between them was that Freya's body was clearly built for power and speed, while Iris's lithe form, while still just as curvaceous, seemed more focused on being graceful and flexible.

As expected of a Regulus Students. Exceptional in every way, Daedalus thought. *I need to hurry up and figure things out so I can start meeting that standard too.*

Daedalus grabbed a towel he was keeping on the floor and wiped off his sweat-drenched face as he walked up to her so he could have a proper conversation. As he neared her, he noticed that she was just as sweaty if not more soaked than he was.

"Thanks again for yesterday," said Daedalus.

"Don't mention it. More importantly, though, the way you fight. That's the same as Prominence's fighting form, isn't it?"

"It is. We both studied the same fighting form, by complete coincidence."

"Interesting. I thought you two may have been childhood friends, which would explain the closeness between you two. But…you say your history is…?"

"Pretty short, honestly. Like, we've technically known each other two years, but we really only interacted with each other for three months a long time ago."

"I find that hard to believe considering how closed off Prominence is. She is extremely resistant to any attempts at familiarity or any sort of real relationship with anyone."

"Yeah, I know. But that's just how it is. I'm not entirely sure why that's the case with me either."

Iris raised an eyebrow. "Perhaps there's something special about you that she sees, but you don't."

"You think so?"

"I would theorize so. I can't speak much on the topic though, since frankly, I don't know anything about you. But if someone like Prominence has opened up to you, there has to be a good reason."

"Maybe it's my sparkling personality and cheerful demeanor, or perhaps my dashing good looks," said Daedalus as he tried to look away with a smoldering intensity.

"You're cute." Iris chuckled. "But just looks wouldn't work on someone like Prominence. Or any Radiant worth their weight in Luvis. You might be able to get in with certain other Radiants with that, but they'll probably just exploit you for sexual services."

"Drat. Oh well, I'll take cute. Gotta take what you can when you're a short stack."

"You're not that short."

"Compared to you and Freya? I'm puny!"

"Well, that's just because we're both abnormally tall."

"I think you mean *perfectly* tall."

"I take it you have a thing for women of high stature?" Iris smirked and crossed her arms. "And I am not referring to status."

"Damn straight. Although, I don't usually verbalize it. Especially around Freya, since it might make things weird," murmured Daedalus, while leaning forward and using one hand as a wall next to his mouth.

"You're peculiar, but I can see how your personality would be entertaining. You seem like a straightforward kind of person. That rare sort of genuine individual. I take it you don't care that Prominence is famous now?"

"Not really. Freya's still Freya. If anything, I was worried she wouldn't talk to me anymore."

"Famous people are still just people. Most of them just want to be treated normally. Not put on pedestals or idolized. Being the center of focus and having such high expectations put on you is its own very intense sort of stress."

"Suffering from success, right?"

Iris's face become stern. "Are you trying to mock me? It wouldn't be the first time I've aired my grievances over this and been laughed at for it. I've heard it all by now, but allow me to say this: success doesn't always equal happiness."

Daedalus shook his head in response as he handed her one of his extra water bottles. "I was being serious. I've seen people become so successful that it becomes a burden. Like a curse. The expectations, the crushing fear of failure that chases them, along with the dread of not living up to the expectations people have put on them... I've never been anywhere near that, but I can see how it'd be overwhelming."

"I see..." Her shoulders relaxing, Iris took the bottle and opened it. "I apologize for immediately taking your comment the wrong way. It seems that you're quite an astute fellow."

"I wouldn't say 'astute.' I just keep an open mind and can understand how people might feel. Truth be told, I think I'm pretty dumb."

"I think you should give yourself some more credit. Empathy is a type of intellect as well. Especially if you can wield it properly."

"Yeah, but it doesn't help me much as a Radiant. What am I going to do? Talk my way to victory with an emotional, heart-wrenching speech? I doubt it." Daedalus chuckled, making an exaggerated Shakespearean pose.

"Perhaps, but there is more to being strong than just having raw power."

Daedalus considered her words for a moment, but couldn't fully grasp what she was trying to say. Power was strength and strength was power. They were both synonyms for each other, so to say that one was more than the other was like saying the number one was more or less than one. Which didn't make sense to him.

"I don't get it."

"I see. Well, perhaps you would like to join me for lunch. I'm quite famished after an intense workout and could use some good company. Eating with others is the seasoning that makes delicious food shine brighter, after all." She smiled.

"Lunch?"

"That's right. That thing people do in the middle of the day? Perhaps you've heard of it before," responded Iris with a smirk.

"You're a sassy one, aren't you?"

"I suppose. Is that a problem?"

"Eh, I've never been one to shy away from the spicier things in life. Including spicy women."

Iris raised an eyebrow. "I've never had someone address me as 'spicy' before. That's a fun turn of phrase. Spicy. I believe that is the most whimsical descriptor that has been tagged onto me. I like it."

"Me too. Burning, intense, and you just can't get enough of it. Nothing beats some quality spicy wings."

"Is that a fact? I've never had the chance to enjoy fingers foods like that before. I'd like to try pizza one day, but my diet doesn't allow it. 'Tis a shame, but the road to greatness isn't an easy one, I'm afraid."

"Hm, Well, if lunch goes well, I know a great place for stuff like that. It'll be our little secret. A little cheat day of sorts," whispered Daedalus with a grin as he prodded the air in Iris's direction with his elbow.

"A cheat day, you say? Hm, that sounds exciting. Very wild."

Iris finished drinking from the water bottle in her hand and skillfully tossed it into the recycling bin before making her way toward the gym showers. At the same time, Daedalus looked at his own clothes and realized that if he was going out, he definitely needed to clean up. So, they agreed to meet in front of the gym after bathing.

CHAPTER 8

The Weakest Guardian

When Daedalus met up with Iris again, she was wearing a floral white summer dress with sandals. The dress reached halfway down her thigh, and she had a stylish belt around her waist that accentuated her curves while emphasizing the sway of her hips as she walked.

On their way to the restaurant for lunch, as soon as they stepped foot off the campus grounds, the first thing they encountered was a small group of protesters. Each one looked just as angry and malicious as the next, but since there were only five, they weren't particularly scary and were easy to ignore. What caught Daedalus's attention the most were their signs, which had all sorts of anti-Radiant propaganda on them. *"Down with Radiants," "Cuff the Uncuffed," "Normal People's Rights Matter Too,"* and more.

After that, Iris was immediately set upon by tons of people who wanted to take photos, get her autograph, shake her hand, or even have her try their products.

"Empress! Empress! Over here! Smile!"

"Empress, can I get a signature?"

"Can you step on me, Empress?"

Daedalus was impressed as he watched Iris deal with the sudden swarm of people surrounding her. All while sipping on a strawberry banana smoothie. They had picked up smoothies near the gym to keep their hunger in check until they could get real food.

She must be famous too. What for? he wondered. *Maybe she's in the top ten for the Amateur League?*

The crowd didn't care much for Daedalus, that was for sure. The hordes of people shoving him around made him lose his previous drink somewhere along his way to the edge of the swarm, far away from Iris.

"It's not every day the Lightning Empress visits the town! Oh! I hope I can get her signature!"

A young girl bounced in place near Daedalus with an admittedly cool-looking picture of Iris in her hands. Iris stood in a powerful pose with an upward camera angle, electricity racing around her, and she wore an outfit that Daedalus found vaguely familiar.

Lightning Empress…I've heard that somewhere.

He tapped his head as he tried to remember where he had heard that moniker before. The fact Iris had a moniker at all was evidence enough that she was an established Radiant, since only the strongest were given nicknames by the organization. Her battle regalia also looked like a professional-grade outfit, which meant the school had gifted it to her for exceptional performance.

"Please, everyone," said Iris. "I'm here to enjoy lunch with a friend. I would love to be able to speak to all of you individually, but would you all be happy with a signature?"

The crowd cheered as Iris lifted up a fine-tipped permanent marker. Then, in the blink of an eye, every single person's things were signed. Iris appeared in front of Daedalus before signing his forehead.

"For you as well." She chuckled.

The electricity sparking off her body had a beautiful, ethereal glow to it. It gave it a more impactful, almost regal appearance that managed to turn on the lightbulb in Daedalus's head.

He snapped his fingers loudly. "I remember now— you're the Radiant who came in second at the Amateur Radiant Grand Championship!"

Iris's eyebrow twitched, but her smile persisted as she took a deep breath before putting away her writing utensil. It was obvious that she was sore over the results of the tournament, but she was doing her best to not let it show.

"T-that's right," she said. "You didn't know who I was until now?"

"Nope! It's cool getting to meet such a powerful Radiant, though. If I remember correctly…you specialize in distance control and long range. And you have a nasty left heel for people who underestimate you and think you're weak in close combat."

"You know a lot about me considering you didn't even know what I looked like."

Daedalus shrugged. "I've read about every Radiant in the leagues so far. I don't really watch them all the time. Not even Freya, embarrassingly enough. Usually, there aren't any pictures, either."

Iris nodded. "I can appreciate that. It's refreshing to meet someone who isn't fawning all over me, to be honest," she said with a smirk. "Or mincing their words to spare my feelings so they don't 'anger' me."

"Happy to oblige."

"Anyway, let's get to the restaurant. Don't want to miss our reservation."

"You made a reservation?" he asked.

"Of course! As a member of the Electra family, I observe all formal rules. Which is why I dressed so nicely for an outing with a gentleman such as yourself. It isn't everyday someone gets to have my undivided attention or view me in such beautiful attire." She brushed her hair over her shoulder.

"I'm honored an—"

Daedalus's attention suddenly shifted, and he stomped the ground right next to Iris, forcing her to take a step away. A sharp cracking sound emanated from under her, and evolved into the noise of a shattering mirror.

"What did you do?" she asked.

"Someone is using Luvis for crappy reasons," he growled, looking around until he spotted the person he was looking for. "Him."

The flow of Luvis from the construct he had crushed originated from a man who was sitting on a low wall, staring at the ground with shock in his eyes. He was holding a camera, and Daedalus knew that it contained a lot of compromising photos due to how long it had taken him to notice the Luvis-based mirror the man had created.

"What do you mean?" said Iris.

"He was using Luvis energy to create a window of sorts. Like a portal, but it can only be used to view one way."

She frowned. "I didn't see or sense anything. Are you sure?"

"I'm certain."

Iris tensed up as she caught on to what he was implying—that someone was using Luvis to look under her skirt. Her eyes became small as electricity crackled to life around her, but before she could say or do anything, Daedalus put his arm up to stop her and marched forward on his own to confront the man.

"Hey! You!" he yelled, catching the man's attention. He looked irritated, no doubt annoyed that somehow his usual trick had been disrupted.

"Whadda you want?" the man snapped, with a toothpick in his mouth as he tried to casually fiddle with his camera.

"Hand over the camera."

"Huh? Are you crazy? Are you trying to rob me in broad daylight?"

Daedalus's hand whipped out and snagged the man's collar before pulling him toward his face. Mere inches away, Daedalus slammed his forehead into his. The man let out a shocked grunt.

"I know you took pictures of Iris."

"The hell are you on, man! I'm a photographer. Taking photos is my job, you stooge!"

"Really? And taking photos under her skirt is part of that job?"

The man tensed up and stumbled while flicking his toothpick around, causing it to fall to the ground. "How the hell would I get photos under her skirt if I've been sitting here this whole time?"

"Seems like a nifty Luvis ability to me," Daedalus growled.

"H—"

"How do I know? Because I saw it. Now, hand over the camera. I'll delete the pictures, and if I *ever* catch you doing this again, I'll personally destroy it and report you to whatever association you sell your photos to."

The man was thrown back against the wall he was sitting on previously, and Daedalus snatched the camera out of his hand to skim through the pictures he had taken. Sure enough, there were countless angles of photos from under Iris's skirt, each one from different stages of her walk. The contrast of her black underwear with the white dress made it especially easy to catch a lot of the finer details.

"So what if I took a few less tasteful pictures? A man's gotta eat, and those sorts of photos fetch a real pretty penny on the market. Don't be trying to be a white knight just to try and get on Iris's good side. You're a nobody to her. She doesn't even notice people like us."

Daedalus ignored the man and deleted every single picture before finally glaring back at the photographer. He didn't say anything else, just tossed the camera back at him.

"I'm not a white knight. I have standards, and nothing pisses me off more than someone misusing Luvis like you have. Luvis is a gift that can be used for great things but also terrible evils for those who don't appreciate it. Although what you did here isn't a "great evil;" it's a pointless, petty disrespect. There's also nothing wrong with making sure the dignity of someone is maintained and that they are given the minimum level of respect that all human beings deserve."

Daedalus's aura flared out, startling the photographer for a moment, but then he seemed underwhelmed by it.

Since the photos were gone, Daedalus took a deep breath to calm himself down before walking back to Iris, who also seemed to have entered a better frame of mind.

"You know, I could have handled him myself," said Iris. Her eyes followed the man as he hurried off.

"You don't need to. Imagine, the famous Iris getting aggressive with someone. Even if it was for good reason, your enemies will weave it into something bad for you and your reputation will suffer for it. Better that a nobody like me handles it. The media can't hurt me like it can hurt you."

"You really are a peculiar fellow."

"So, still on for lunch?"

"Of course."

Iris took the lead as Daedalus walked a few steps behind her. His guard was up, and he kept a close eye on any Luvis activity in their vicinity to make sure it wasn't malicious. His behavior made Iris smile a bit, as if she enjoyed the way he was trying to protect her.

CHAPTER 9

The Lunch

"I'd like to have the chicken panini. Thank you."

"Hm. I'll have the Cuban sandwich. Sliced pickles, please."

After making it to the café admittedly late, Iris and Daedalus were both eager to order their foods so that they could take the edge off their increasing hunger. The waitress who took their order was at first starstruck when she noticed Iris, but she quickly regained her professional composure to take their orders.

"So, a Cuban?"

"Yup."

"A tasteful sandwich choice."

"And tasty."

Iris fiddled with the tea she had ordered as Daedalus took a sip of his soda. He sensed she was trying to find a way to start a more meaningful conversation, but for some reason or another, she was having trouble finding a good topic.

"E-excuse me, I—I have a Cuban and the chicken panini?"

A shorter woman with messy black hair and a cute waitressing dress approached their table with an awkward smile on her face. She held a plate in each hand, but Daedalus noticed she seemed to be struggling to balance them on her palm.

Just as he was about to offer to help, it happened.

"Ah!"

First it was his Cuban; it tumbled through the air as if in slow motion, flying straight at Iris. Almost immediately after, due to the waitress's spastic attempt to catch the already dropped sandwich, Iris's panini went hurtling at Daedalus. It was a tragic series of events. As the food splattered on them, the girl looked on in horror, her hands gripping the sides of her hair.

"I'm so sorry! Oh, my goodness!" she cried.

"It's fine."

"Talk about express delivery." Daedalus chuckled.

Iris casually picked up the fallen plate and started taking parts of the Cuban sandwich off of herself. As she took off more of the food covering her from head to toe, it was soon revealed that the mustard from the sandwich had stained a good portion of her white dress.

"Hm. This was part of the special collection too." She sighed. "Oh well."

At the same time, Daedalus was also picking off the panini from his clothes, but whenever he found an intact piece of food, his instincts made him eat it. This earned him an amused look from Iris once she noticed.

"No food wasted mindset, I take it?" she asked, as she lifted up some pork and ate it. "Noble, although almost too wild for me. Yet, I will join you, because I'm feeling rebellious today."

"I'll get you replacements right away!" said the waitress. "I'm so sorry!"

The girl continued apologizing as Iris took a bite of some bread she had previously put on the plate and let out a small giggle. The novelty and ridiculousness of what she was doing amused her, but after another second, she cleared her throat to address the waitress.

"Of course. Pay no mind. Everyone makes mistakes." She smiled.

"Yeah, besides, now that I've had a bite of chicken, I think I'll want a panini too," said Daedalus.

"I was about to request a change of my panini to the Cuban." Iris giggled. "I suppose we are so hungry that our cravings shifted with the first thing we ate."

The two laughed, and the waitress seemed to calm down slightly due to how well they were taking the accident. With a small bow, she picked up the mess that was now contained to the plate and ran off back to the kitchen.

"Your blouse is stained." Daedalus pointed at it.

"I know. It's a shame. I was quite fond of this dress."

"I bet. It really makes you 'pop,' you know?"

Iris looked down at the stain, but when she heard what Daedalus said, she lifted an eyebrow as a wicked smile spread on her lips.

"No, I'm afraid I don't. Would you care to elaborate?" she asked, looking to tease him a bit.

"I mean, the dress makes you like…Boom! And bam!"

Daedalus made explosion motions over his chest, while genuinely explaining what he meant. Iris crossed her arms with surprise on her face, as if he'd spoiled part of her fun.

"You have no filter, do you?" she said.

"Probably not. Besides, did you really think I'd fall for such obvious bait?"

"Ah—I…wasn't trying to…"

"But you were," countered Daedalus, wiggling his finger at her with a grin. "I'm not going to get flustered over something like that. If you asked me, 'Do I look good in this,' I would have probably told you that I was expecting a snack to accompany me to lunch, not an eight-course meal."

"Hahaha!"

Iris burst out laughing. A big smile rose on her face that differed from her usual, formal smile. It looked much more natural, and at the same time, Daedalus felt that it suited her much better.

"What?" he asked.

"You'd use such obviously flirtatious sentences so casually?" she said, while trying to catch her breath.

"I mean, I'm just being honest, and I'm not so boring as to be like, 'Oh yeah, you look good.' Or, 'You look great.' If I'm going to give a compliment, might as well take it the whole nine yards. You know?"

"You are definitely not boring. Although, most men would keep it basic when getting to know someone. Is that your philosophy? Going all in all day?"

"Basically. Try as hard as possible, do the best I can in everything. Never leave room for regrets. Even when I brush my teeth, I make sure these babies sparkle like pearls."

Daedalus lifted up part of his lip to reveal beautifully white, shining teeth. In response, Iris brought her own finger up to mimic him, but hesitated for a few seconds before finally replicating the action.

"I too am an enjoyer of proper dental hygiene."

"It shows. Those are some mighty fine chompers. Matches the set perfectly."

"The set?"

"When taking into account everything about you, the quality of your teeth match everything else perfectly," elaborated Daedalus, with a finger pointing up matter-of-factly.

By now, the series of unusual compliments had started taking effect on Iris, and a blush rose on her cheeks. In order to regain her composure, she took a deep breath and rubbed her cheeks before placing her hands on the table neatly.

"I see that you are also a master of wordplay. Are you perhaps trying to win me over? I would assume that is the case, because your words are too powerful for mere casual talk. Then again, it seems you are perhaps *too* well-versed in the art of words in winning a maiden's affections. It makes me slightly weary."

"You think so? I think you're giving me too much credit. I don't think you realize how easy you make it to compliment you."

"I am aware. It's just that your boldness and uniqueness when weaving words is not something I have come across before. Especially not with such a lighthearted, casual air. Most men who even remotely match you are obviously filled with lust and other unsavory intentions."

"Sounds like you need to find more quality men to talk to." Daedalus shrugged and took a sip of his soda.

"Perhaps you're right." Iris chuckled.

"I-I'm sorry for the wait! Here are your orders!"

The waitress made her way carefully once again toward them with their food in hand. This time, she was accompanied by a second waitress who was acting as a sort of safeguard to make sure nothing got dropped a second time.

"Fantastic! I'm dying."

Daedalus slumped onto the table comically. His plate was placed right next to him. Then, Iris got her sandwich.

"Thank you," they both said in unison, and the two waitresses left. The first one still looked extremely apologetic about what had happened.

"See, I told you it was easy, Clara! Cheer up!" said the second waitress, comforting the first as they returned to the kitchen.

"Well," said Iris, "I suppose now it is time to dig in! The wait and enjoyable conversation have left me even more famished than I was before I came here. It's quite wild!"

Iris picked up her Cuban and rotated it around to examine it before she took a bite. As she chewed, she let out a soft squeal, and Daedalus couldn't help but smile as he took a bite of his own panini.

The two ate together in silence, but there was no more awkwardness. It had become a quietness of two people who were enjoying each other's company with quality food. An event that needed no words other than the occasional hum of enjoyment as they feasted.

* * *

Following the end of their meal, Iris excused herself, saying that she had something important to attend to soon and that she didn't want to be late for it. With a wave of her hand, she left, but not before inviting Daedalus out for another "food outing" whenever his schedule would allow for it.

Daedalus stopped by the grocery store to grab the ingredients for his famous ramen, and then he headed back to the dorm and plopped himself on the couch to watch some television. There wasn't anything he was particularly interested in, though, so he eventually fell asleep until the sound of the door opening woke him up.

Daedalus's eyes fluttered open, and he tried to get up from the couch. But before he could, a shirt fell over his face and he heard the sounds of pants being unzipped. Which was promptly followed by the sound of jeans being tossed onto the floor.

"Hey, Freya… I'm here, you know…"

He tried to remind Freya that he was in the dorm room, but because he'd just woken up, his voice was still soft and deep. It didn't project very well through the shirt covering his face. So, he lifted himself off the couch and pulled the shirt off before trying again.

"Oooy."

Freya turned toward him as she was in the middle of heading to her room. By that point, the only things she had on were her bra and underwear, both in a beautiful pink hue with golden accents.

She didn't say anything; in fact, she didn't even react to the fact Daedalus was there. Instead, Freya just blinked once and then sauntered off into her room as if she hadn't seen anything, but made sure to gently close her door.

That's…odd.

Daedalus didn't really know what her reaction meant, although he knew that he had been blessed to see her majestic visage. He was sure no other man had gotten the privilege of observing it. At the same time, seeing her half naked wasn't anything terribly new to him. Still, it was a breathtaking sight each time.

I guess Freya still doesn't care if I see her like that. On that note, I should start making the ramen.

Daedalus jumped up from the couch and went to the kitchen to put together what he needed to make his famous ramen.

A few minutes later, he heard a series of muted squeaks followed by a door opening.

"So, like, five…ten minutes it'll be ready," called out Daedalus.

"Thanks."

The squeaking continued to the rhythm of walking as it grew closer. In fact, it continued for so long that Daedalus couldn't help but turn away from his pot so that he could locate the source. His eyes fell upon a familiar figure dressed in an animal onesie.

Donning an orange-and-white tiger onesie, complete with an eared hoodie, Freya was pushing her feet, stuffed into big tiger booties, against the floor. This action was causing the squeaking sound that Daedalus had been hearing, but now that he knew the source, he couldn't help but find it more cute than annoying.

"What?"

Freya finally noticed Daedalus's gaze, and she brought her feet together up on the couch.

"Uh. Nothing, I just…when did you get that?"

"Two years ago."

"I see. It's cute."

"Thanks."

"Now you match Mr. Tora."

Freya brightened up, the ears of her hood wiggling slightly. She adjusted herself in her seat. "You remember Mr. Tora?"

"How could I not?" replied Daedlaus, with a moderately offended expression. "He's your best friend, after all."

"Yeah."

She gained a small smile and wiggled her knees. Apparently, whatever had been bothering her before was no longer on her mind. With a full-body hop, she turned to poke her head over the couch to look at the pot.

"Is it ready?" she asked, her hips swaying. She looked like a cute tiger getting ready to pounce into the kitchen.

"Almost. I added extra chipotle, just how you like it."

Daedalus walked back to the kitchen and tasted the broth. He smacked his lips a few times to get a good sense of the flavor profile, and when he felt that it was perfect, he took out two bowls from the cabinet.

"One for the hungry tiger," said Daedalus. He turned around to see that Freya had tried to paw the air in anticipation without being caught. She stopped mid-swipe and looked away with the color rising in her cheeks. "And one for me."

The aroma from the modified instant ramen was smokey and fragrant, courtesy of the chipotle. On top of that, the broth held an enticing dark red hue to it, given vibrant life due to the added green garnishes and the white noodles bundled up in the middle.

"Soup's on!"

Daedalus grabbed both bowls and placed them on the table, which caused Freya to start bouncing eagerly in place. He handed her a spoon and turned on the TV.

"Movie?"

Freya nodded as she took a sip of the broth. She shivered in glee when the flavors hit her tongue.

"Even better than I remember."

"You think so?"

"Mhm."

Even though Freya was terrible at expressing herself with her face, Daedalus could still see how she was feeling based on how her Luvis fluctuated around her and her body language. That was why he knew how much she was enjoying the ramen, and that something had definitely been bothering her earlier when she entered the dorm. He just didn't know what.

"Oh, I love *Job-full Rebirth*!"

Daedalus took a seat next to Freya, and they both ate while watching TV. Chewing and slurping in silence, there wasn't much else for them to do, and by the end of their meal, they both ended up falling asleep on the couch together, with Freya's fluffy onesie acting like a pillow for Daedalus.

CHAPTER 10

Radiant Amateur League

A shockwave exploded outward as Daedalus's fist met Freya's, and the two quickly disengaged before crashing into each other with mirrored kicks. The battle had begun in a flash, with an unexpected level of ferocity between the two fighters.

Luvis flared outward, bursting to life like a sea of energy. Daedalus deftly maneuvered around Freya, his eyes burning a blazing blue. Like a shark, he navigated through the sea of Luvis surrounding him with an ease that left Freya baffled. She had never seen someone moving the way he was, and while it seemed similar to Striking Tiger Palm, it was vastly different in many ways.

Once again, the two crashed with their forearms, but Daedalus shoved forward powerfully, blowing Freya back in a shocking display of strength. Her eyes widened in shock. She'd never expected to be knocked back by Daedalus, whose Luvis was so much weaker than hers.

Regardless of her respect for him as a person, it was a fact that his Luvis was nothing compared to hers, and in combat, it was supposed to be painfully obvious how this discrepancy created an advantage. But somehow, Daedalus had learned to keep pace with her. A small smile tugged at her mouth.

The two clashed kicks again, but this time Daedalus forced her leg down before he threw a kick into her abdomen. He followed this move with a roundhouse kick that she managed to catch at the last second.

Daedalus's feet were blazing with a blue Luvis-fueled fire, and he moved them with a deftness that hinted at how much time and effort he had put into practicing his combat techniques. Still, even that shouldn't have been enough to allow him to catch up to Freya in any meaningful way.

"Not bad." She smiled.

Once again, Daedalus forced his way through her block, but Freya jumped back just in time and dropped into a deep crouch as her hair exploded into a fiery, golden mane.

Vanishing in an explosion of wind, golden light, and debris, Freya closed the gap between her and Daedalus at a speed faster than even most Luvis-enhanced eyes could track. With her legs brought up to her chest, she appeared horizontal right in front of Daedalus and, with a powerful kick, sent him crashing into the matted wall.

"Gah!"

Daedalus landed on the ground and brushed off the blow, as if it wasn't anything special, and he began running close to the ground while remaining on two feet.

"How do you like my impromptu style?" he asked.

Getting near Freya, he twisted around and whipped his heel out. The attack barely missed Freya, who leaned back. The brightness of the foot near her face suddenly intensified, and she was temporarily blinded.

This created an opening for Daedalus's other leg as he quickly repositioned himself to let loose a second kick, which caught Freya's side. He used that to twist his body once more and landed a back roundhouse on her neck.

"Ow."

Freya crashed to the floor, but recovered with a graceful series of twists and a backhand spring that left her no worse for wear. She was pleasantly surprised at how she was being outdone in terms of technique. She liked a challenge.

Daedalus didn't give her room to appreciate his progress over the past two years. He continued his non-stop, relentless assault against her. At the same time, Freya couldn't help but notice that his ferocity seemed to have a controlled, almost calm element to it. Unlike the traditional Striking Tiger Palm move, it felt more tactical and analytical. Which made it feel like she was fighting a lion rather than a tiger. She also found it peculiar how most of his attacks centered around using his legs more than his arms, which was the usual main focus of the style.

Small thuds resonated out from where Daedalus's leg met Freya's block. She was watching carefully now with a sharp eye to catch every single movement he made, so that she could eventually read his intentions. Even so, she was having trouble understanding his new fighting form. She continued blocking using not just her arms, but also her legs.

"Ferocious," praised Freya.

She threw herself back as she dodged one last heel from Daedalus, and with a backflip in midair, she stuck her landing only to vanish once again.

This time, she changed her attack pattern. Daedalus was suddenly hit from various different angles in the same instant, forcing him to fall onto his knee.

"Ow...ow...ow...ow."

"Sorry, did I go too hard?" said Freya, appearing in front of Daedalus with her hands hovering over him.

"No, it's fine. Wow, that smarts. It's the only thing I haven't figured out how to counter yet."

"What do you mean?"

"I bet you're wondering how I'm able to keep up with you better than before, right?" said Daedalus, jumping to his feet.

"It's not just technical skill?"

"No, I actually figured out a way to focus my Luvis. It's the reverse of the principle we tried creating originally for your aura, before we decided it'd be easier to just stretch it out as far as possible. Using this technique, even with my bad capacity and potency of Luvis, I can concentrate it to become just as useful as yours. Not to mention, the more I concentrate it, the more powerful it becomes. For example...my finger!"

Daedalus brought up his pointer finger and wiggled it.

"If I concentrate all my Luvis to the tip of my finger, I can virtually block anything. Although, if I block incorrectly by even a little bit, I'm basically screwed. Which is the other problem—because my Luvis is concentrated in the one spot, the rest of me is defenseless. So, if an attack hits me from all around at the same time, I'm toast."

"Ah."

"Yeah." He grimaced. "I'm working on it, but this trick has helped a lot. It requires a lot of focus, though, because I need to be able to move this tiny little concentrated dot of Luvis all around my body so it can absorb attacks or be used to attack. Then again, for attacks I tend to make the concentration more generalized...like my feet."

He brought a foot up and wiggled it in the air.

Freya crossed her arms as a thoughtful expression came across her face. "Have you thought about joining the Amateur League?"

"I mean, even if I wanted to, I can't. Only freshmen who rank in the top three of their Orientation Tournaments are considered. Usually, only champions are allowed instant access."

The Radiant Amateur League was the "little brother" to the Professional League. It acted as a sort of preview league that allowed people to see who the next big Radiants were going to be in the world. It took a certain level of Radiant to be allowed into the RAL in the first place, which kept the matches exciting and to a certain standard. It was also necessary to be of a certain ranking inside the RAL to be considered for the Professional League.

"I can recommend you," offered Freya.

"You can do that?"

She nodded. "As the Champion, I have a lot of benefits I usually don't use. One of them is giving a free pass into the RAL for anyone I deem "capable." Of course, they will fall under the same rules as everyone else, so if they underperform well below the standards, they will be kicked out."

"Hm." Daedalus stroked his chin, considering. "Do you think I'd stand a good chance in the RAL?"

"I think so. Not many keep up as well as you did with me, even in the RAL."

"Yeah, but you aren't even trying your hardest."

"I rarely do. Only during major tournaments in the semi-finals do I have to put effort in. No offense."

"None taken. I'd be toast if you went all out, haha."

What Freya was hoping for was that with time in real combat, within the RAL, Daedalus's growth as a Radiant would accelerate. It was admittedly impressive that he'd managed to grow as much as he did on his own, but the things a person could learn in real-time combat were far beyond what could be achieved through just practice. This was something she had learned quickly when she had entered the RAL, and Freya was certain she wouldn't have become as powerful as she currently was if she hadn't battled with others all out for two years.

In a similar fashion, Freya had high hopes that the combat of the RAL would help not only improve Daedalus's already impressive quick-thinking and prediction skills but also help him learn new techniques that would make him even more powerful. After all, his unique skill he was using now was based off just a short three months of theory crafting for a mostly unrelated problem.

A shudder of excitement ran through her at how much Daedalus would learn and improve within the RAL. Also, at how much of a fun and enjoyable opponent he'd be once he eventually entered the same realm of strength as her, which she had no doubt he would. In fact, she felt that he might be able to catch up to her in less than a year's time, considering his personality.

"Even if I want to join, I'll have to wait until next year, since that's going to be my next chance," said Daedalus.

Radiants who didn't qualify for the RAL their freshman year were left with no other choice but to wait one full school year. Once in their sophomore year, with a teacher recommendation, they'd be allowed to try to enter once more, but Regulus was well known for being extremely strict when it came to faculty recommendations.

"Not if I give you my recommendation," said Freya.

Daedalus puffed out his cheeks as he put a finger to his forehead, clearly tempted by her offer, but hesitating for some reason. She figured he felt like he would be somehow cheating. So, she prodded him again. "You shouldn't pass up a good opportunity when it's presented to you."

"Well, if you're going to believe in me that much, I guess I have no choice but to accept." Daedalus grinned as he re-entered a fighting stance. "Which also means I need to train even harder, so I won't make you look bad for recommending me."

"I don't think that's a possibility." Freya smiled too, gently, as she brought her own fists up.

* * *

A week passed as Daedalus figured out the paperwork he needed to fill out. After scheduling an appointment for the hearing regarding his potential entry into the RAL, he and Freya were able to head to the President's office for the final decision. Both were confident it would be a yes due to Freya's authority as the RAL Champion.

"No."

Daedalus and Freya looked at each other in alarm.

"What do you mean no?" he asked.

"I said, *no*."

Frederika sat on the school President's desk, with a nonchalant but serious air about her as she chewed on a lollipop. She still had her sunglasses on, and it seemed that she wasn't going to budge on the topic of allowing

Daedalus into the Radiant Amateur League, despite Freya's recommendation.

"I can allow him in," argued Freya, a small frown on her face.

"Yes, technically, but it needs to be approved. And I don't approve."

"You aren't President Alice."

"Perhaps not, but I am second-in-command around these parts…unofficially. Besides, that isn't the problem. This man, Daedalus Notos, I remember him from when you two first applied. You're good friends with him. I can respect helping your friends, and I can respect his tenacity to finally get accepted, but don't you think it's dangerous to put him in a place where he doesn't belong? He's going to get hurt in the RAL. Just look at his charts. He's ranked in the middle of his tournament. His third tournament. He just barely made the cut-off."

Frederika brought out a folder from behind Alice's desk and handed it to Freya.

"He's going to get badly injured and get kicked out, maybe even crippled. And it'll be on you for trying to play favorites. The privilege of the Champion is to make competition more exciting by finding diamonds in the rough. Not to abuse it to bring along friends." Frederika glared at Freya.

"He can do it."

"Tell you two what," said Frederika with a smirk." If you can get a recommendation from another high-ranking Radiant in the RAL, I'll allow it."

Daedalus held back a grin. This was going to be easy. "So, someone like the Lightning Empress?" he asked.

"Yes, a Radiant of her level would meet the criteria. After all, she is second only to Gold Prominence here. Good luck getting her approval, though, or even just getting in contact with her."

"I have her on speed dial," said Daedalus, taking his phone out of his pocket.

"What?" said Freya and Frederika in simultaneous confusion.

"I mean, I only really have like four contacts. One of them is Freya, and I have her on speed dial too. It only makes sense." He chuckled as his phone rang. Then, someone picked up on the other side. "Hey…yeah. Yeah, no. Next week's still fine. Yeah. Well, actually, I wanted to know if you could come down to the President's office. No, I'm not in trouble. Yeah, if it isn't too much of a hassle… Great. Thanks!"

Daedalus pocketed his phone and looked up to see a flabbergasted Frederika and a mildly suspicious Freya.

"Who did you just call?" demanded Frederika.

"Who do you think?"

"How do you have Electra's number?" asked Freya, crossing her arms.

"We've had lunch a few times, and she just gave me her number after the third time so it'd be easier to schedule them and get in contact if something comes up. You know?"

Freya looked at Frederika, who got up from leaning on the desk and marched up to Daedalus with a vicious smirk.

"Quite the player, aren't you? You've managed to get in the good graces of not just Gold Prominence but also the Lightning Empress? What gives?"

"Uh…being a decent person? Is it really that odd to be friends with someone?"

"No, but befriending those two is. Not only do they not get along very well, but their personalities are vastly different. How can one person be of a character that they both agree with?"

"How should I know? Right, Freya?"

Freya gave him a long look, then let out a sigh and dropped her arms to her side.

"It's not so strange…" she admitted. "Daedalus is…a good man."

Frederika whipped her whole body around and almost gave herself whiplash to face Freya, as if she couldn't believe what she was hearing. After several long moments, her strong glare aimed straight at Daedalus, like she was examining him, trying to figure out what was so "good" about him. But before she could say anything else, the door to the office opened.

"I'm here. What seems to be the matter?"

Iris strutted in, surveyed the room, and casually walked over to Frederika with her hands on her hips.

"This man is interested in joining the RAL," said Frederika. "He has Prominence's recommendation, but I won't acknowledge it without your approval as well."

"Why is that? The Champion holds that right, don't they?" asked Iris, turning to face Freya.

"Because he is a known ally of Prominence. It is dangerous to allow him into the RAL," countered Frederika. "He will be a danger to himself and ruin the school's reputation *and* Prominence's."

"A fair argument." Iris looked Daedalus up and down, and he gave her a hopeful smile. "As fond as I am of him, I can't simply give my approval, as I'm sure Stryker is aware. Although, I doubt she is giving her approval on a whim or just on their friendship either."

Daedalus's face fell. *Really? She's not gonna help me?*

"Regardless, my condition is set," said Frederika. "Which means his request is denied without your recommendation."

Iris held up a hand. "Hold on, Instructor. Before I give my official verdict, I'd like an opportunity to battle him. To see for myself the true breadth of his skill and if there is true weight to his recommendation. If he has a reason to be in the RAL, I see no reason to deny him, and I think we will all see that reason through a simple match."

Frederika sniffed distastefully. "If you insist. But if I see that you are holding back, I will end the match and outright deny his request," she added with a threatening glare as she pulled out another lollipop from her blazer.

"I wouldn't dream of it," said Iris. "Not only would that be insulting to you and the school, but it would also be an extraordinary disrespect to Daedalus here. I would be besmirching my honor and nobility with such an act, as well as hurting others in many ways."

Iris fanned her hair out gracefully, and Frederika nodded as she made her way to the door.

"Then let's get this over with."

CHAPTER 11

The Lightning Empress

"I will serve as the witness to this match," declared Frederika, who was sitting lazily on the podium. "The match will continue until one side is unable to keep going or surrenders. Is that clear?"

Iris and Daedalus both nodded.

Right after the meeting in the office, the group had headed toward one of the arenas. Iris had changed into a pair of shorts and a sports bra that gave her the maximum movement available. Similarly, Daedalus had changed into a tight white athletic shirt and shorts.

"Hey, hey, hey!" a cute voice piped up, seemingly from right next to them.

Frederika tensed up for a moment, then stood up straighter, with more pride in her stance. Not long after, the sound of small steps echoed through the arena. Daedalus turned his head as President Alice hopped onto the battlefield with a spin before vanishing and appearing next to Frederika.

"Hey, hey!" she repeated while fixing a small hat on her head. "I heard that Frederika was being mean!"

"I'm upholding the honor and integrity of Regu—"

"Boo boo!" Alice interrupted Frederika by throwing her finger up and making a pouting face. "You made a decision without me, Rika! That's so mean!"

"I—"

"I know you mean well Rika, but you need to be nicer to the students. They have aspirations…dreams! If they want to risk it all to grab them, we should encourage them, not be unnecessary obstacles!"

"I understand that but, in this case I—"

"I've heard all about the situation from my secretary. If this young man wants to push himself, allow him to show us his worth. Even if it might lead to disastrous results for him."

The final words from Alice's mouth came off as oddly sinister, and a chill ran down Daedalus's spine. But her beaming smile never left her lips as she pulled out her signature mic stand from behind the podium. She skipped happily up to Daedalus, then suddenly stopped and tilted her head when she got a closer look at him.

"Yes?" he asked, rather uncomfortable.

Alice let out a long "Hm" as if she was deep in thought, and then she jumped back and poked Daedalus's cheek gently with the end of her mic stand.

"Ah! You're Emilia's son, aren't you?" she declared loudly.

"Uh...yeah? How do you know my mom?"

"Oh, you're just like her! Even as a youngster, she was always so rebellious. She pulled off something wack-a-doodle like this when she went to school, too. I remember because I always got caught up in the aftermath of her shenanigans..."

"Wack-a-doodle?"

"You take right after your mom! How is she? Is she doing all right?"

"My mom...died."

Daedalus felt his head get pushed back as Alice prodded his cheek more.

"I know that, silly. Haven't you visited her grave? Made sure it's okay?"

"I visit once a year."

"Good!"

"I'd still like to know, how do you know my mom?" he asked. "She never went to Regulus."

Alice spun her cane before hopping up onto the podium and grabbing Frederika by her blazer collar. She yanked her back to bring her onto the floating podium, seemingly ignoring Daedalus's question.

"Emilia and I are old friends, even though she always gave me a lot of trouble," said Alice, slumping over in an exaggerated way. "More importantly, if you are her son, that makes things a lot more fun. It seems you inherited Emilia's annoying charisma, too…although, you don't seem as physically attractive." She frowned at him. "Your dad must be pretty average. Weird."

"Uh…"

Daedalus didn't know how to take Alice's words, since she was simultaneously insulting and praising his parents, but he decided it was better to just stay silent in the current situation.

"Anyways! I want to see if Emilia's legacy is strong in you." Alice smiled. "Show me what you've got! If you impress me, regardless of whether you win or not, I'll allow you to join the RAL. Then again, Iris here is definitely a tough cookie. It will be hard to show off your stuff with her. You would've been better off trying to seduce her to get her approval rather than fighting her, haha!"

"A noble lady wouldn't let something like carnal desire sway their judgement," said Iris, her hands on her hips.

Alice patted the air in front of her as if she was patting the top of Iris's head. "Right, right. Anyways, whenever you two are ready, get to it!"

The podium jumped high into the air with a tap from Alice's cane, leaving Daedalus and Iris alone on the battlefield.

* * *

In the distance, Freya watched intently to see how the battle would go. Realistically, she knew that Daedalus wasn't going to win, but she was curious to see how he would fare against a new opponent of equally high status as herself. How well he'd adapt and if he could earn the respect of everyone watching.

"I'm going to go all out," declared Iris, explosive electricity bursting to life around her. "Don't die on me! Show me what got Stryker to give you her support aside from an attractive face."

Iris swung an arm forward, and electricity snaked around her body until it began shooting out of her finger at absurd speeds. With one hand, Daedalus blocked the attack; it scattered as soon as it hit his palm, much to everyone's surprise. Except Freya.

That's his concentration. His Luvis is so dense the current can't pass through it.

The electricity being deflected off of Daedalus's palm quickly redirected into the ground around him as the attack continued. After a few seconds, Iris seemed to realize she wasn't going to make any progress that way. So, she slammed both hands into the ground and sent a wave of lightning down the battlefield straight at Daedalus.

This time, he rammed his shoulder into the wave, scattered the lightning into the air, and not even Freya knew how he managed to do it.

"Hm. What an interesting use of Luvis," said Iris, flexing her hand. "You use the same forms as Stryker, yet you display different abilities. Even she wouldn't try to brute force my lightning, yet you seem completely unaffected. How?"

"It's a secret." Daedalus smiled.

* * *

What Daedalus hadn't told anyone, not even Freya, was that concentrating Luvis wasn't the only thing he had learned how to do. Along the way, he had also managed to figure out how to disrupt Luvis-based attacks by pushing his own Luvis through their flow. Effectively disturbing the delicate structures and breaking whatever form an attack was currently taking.

It wasn't a terribly fancy or grandiose ability, but it was one made possible due to his ability to see Luvis. This allowed him to find the best places to push his Luvis through to destroy the attack and scatter it back into normal Luvis energy. Daedalus was nervous about it, though, because he had yet to test the ability against truly powerful Luvis-based attacks.

If I mess up, I'm toast, but as long as she thinks I can indefinitely beat her lightning, she'll hopefully transition into martial arts. I think I can win there...

There was a brief pop in the air as Iris vanished in a storm of lightning. The thunderclap generated by her movement buffeted Daedalus despite him being a good distance away from her; his ears were ringing.

A powerful knee crashed into his stomach as he tried to regain his footing. Electricity surged throughout his body, sending him away with such force that the moment he touched the ground, he bounced off it and did a full, involuntary flip before crashing back into the floor.

"Whatever skill you're using doesn't seem to work in close combat. Or perhaps you assumed I wasn't good in melee range?" said Iris with a smirk.

"Didn't really expect it..." Daedalus groaned, slowly getting back up. "Electra style users usually like staying away..."

"That's what makes me different...and more dangerous."

Iris kicked the ground and sent a torrent of lightning at Daedalus, but because he was still recovering from that single knee, he took the full force of the attack, which knocked him back even farther.

* * *

Up on the floating podium, Frederika sighed. "I suppose this match is over," she said, looking on with disinterest.

"I wouldn't count him out yet." Alice chuckled. "He's Emilia's son, after all. She was one stubborn woman. I can only imagine how hardheaded he is."

* * *

The electricity surged through Daedalus's body, but within a second, he had managed to force disperse it back into Luvis. He stood up just in time to see Iris's fist coming toward him, but in a surprising turn of events, he managed to dodge the blow. Then, he grabbed her wrist to throw her over his shoulder and slam her onto the floor.

"Gah!"

Iris's body sparked with vicious electricity. Before it could do anything, though, Daedalus firmly punched her sternum and scattered all of it, much to her shock.

How does he keep doing that?

Left with no other choice but to fight without her ability activating, Iris threw her legs into the air with the intent to hit Daedalus's. When she missed, she quickly brought her legs apart and used her hands to rapidly spin while staying in a low handstand.

Now confronting a hurricane of kicks, Daedalus tried to block them, but his guard was easily knocked away and he took two powerful kicks to the face. They left him disoriented and open to multiple other fearsome kicks.

With Daedalus properly off balance, Iris took the opportunity to quickly jump back onto her feet, and without wasting a moment, she landed a powerful punch in Daedalus's stomach. Crouched down, she threw a fearsome rotating kick into his gut and then kept him in place by fluidly jumping up into a beautiful diagonal axe kick.

"Ngh!"

Daedalus's body tensed up after the last kick, and it seemed like he was going to fall, but Iris didn't wait around to see if he would finally buckle. She used the full reach of her long legs to hit Daedalus's chin and jumped forward with a back kick to close the gap before unleashing a flurry of powerful, relentless punches all across his body.

The force of the blows, even without the electricity, was enough to severely jar Daedalus, who wasn't expecting such a fluid and seemingly endless combo from Iris. The strength of her fists was so intense that each blow resonated deeply within his skull, leaving him unable to even act on reflex as his brain bounced around in his head.

Iris smiled, satisfied, seeing the look on his face. It was clear he was realizing that his hubris had gotten the better of him. He had underestimated her abilities, even though she had ranked second in the RAL Championship. It should have been a given that she was every bit a close combat master as Freya.

* * *

"He's just a punching bag at this point," said Frederika, examining her fingernails.

"He's not done yet," said Alice, an amused smile on her face. Her eyes seemed to be reminiscing over something. "This is usually where she would blow her lid. Watch."

* * *

Sure enough, Daedalus let out a defiant roar, but Iris at this point was looking to close the battle up like she would in any other match.

She jumped high into the air with an electrical burst. She then twisted powerfully while suspended in midair, and with a backward outstretched claw hand, she formed a powerful bolt of electricity that stretched nearly a quarter across the length of the field.

"This won't kill you, Daedalus. But it isn't going to tickle, either. Brace yourself!"

Daedalus gulped as he weighed his chances at being able to dispel an attack of that level. Doing it to her more standard lighting attacks wasn't difficult due to how simplistic they were in nature, but this attack that was blazing light across the whole arena was obviously a different beast.

This is going to really, really suck.

Iris let loose the attack without further delay. A terrifying thunderclap rattled the whole building as her hand threw the lightning bolt forward, and it raced through the air despite its big size. Without much time to think, Daedalus relied on the one thing he could.

"No…way."

"That's…impossible."

"Hahahaha!"

Alice burst out laughing up in the podium, while pointing, as Daedalus threw an arm up and lifted a single finger to block Iris's attack. The moment the tip of the electric spear touched his finger, it stopped. It became a battle of an unstoppable force against an immovable object. Frederika was staring wide-eyed with such surprise that her sunglasses almost slid off her face, and Iris's face held the same amount of shock as she stayed floating in the air.

"He's...blocking it with one finger? That's absurd," cried Iris.

To everyone watching, it looked like he was performing an act of unbelievable power and strength, but in reality, it was taking every single last bit of his energy to layer his Luvis continuously so that it formed a strong layer of Luvis that the bolt couldn't pierce.

It was a poor situation to be in, but the only idea he'd had left. If his concentration faltered for even a millisecond, or if his Luvis stopped layering correctly, the full force of the attack was going to hit him. He wasn't sure if his body, without Luvis protection, would survive that sort of attack.

He couldn't even deflect the attack or disperse it either, due to not having enough Luvis. And because the area blocking the tip of the spear was so miniscule, even his blood pumping in his finger ran the very real risk of throwing off the delicate balance he had managed to strike.

This stings like a bitch! Holy smokes!

Daedalus kept his will firm and refused to back down out of principle, and because he was unsure if he would be okay if he let it hit him. But after so much time blocking the electric attack, his arm was starting to become seriously damaged from the downward force and random electric arcs.

Out of nowhere, a powerful blast of golden energy crashed into the spear of electricity, destroying it with a loud explosion that sent Daedalus flying across the floor.

* * *

On the podium, Frederika looked at Freya in alarm. "Why are you interfering with—"

"It's fine," said Alice. She kept Frederika in her place by placing her arm in front of her. "It seems that Freya Stryker has a softer side and keener eye than expected."

"What do you mean?"

"Don't worry about it, Rika!"

* * *

Iris dropped to the ground and ran over to Daedalus, who was sweating heavily while clutching his arm. The attack hadn't hit him, but judging by the state of his arm, one would believe it had. Lacerations and blood were abundant over his right arm, and Daedalus was trying to control his breathing to manage the pain radiating through his body.

"These are pretty bad. I'm so sorry! I got carried away!" cried Iris.

"Yeah, it was pretty...ngh...cool...though, right?" Daedalus chuckled with a weak smile, trying to fight through the immense pain in his limb.

"What was?"

"Blocking...that...awesome attack...with one finger!"

"I—I guess, but look at you now! If Stryker hadn't dispersed it, you'd be a lot worse off. I'm so sorry!"

"W-well. You did say...you were going all out. Hehe...besides, it's fine. This is good. D...don't apologize. It's not like this is my first time getting hurt."

Daedalus tried getting up, but dropped flat onto the floor again, still holding his arm. He rolled onto his back and gave Iris a wink. The world was turning black around him; he was losing consciousness.

* * *

Daedalus's attitude in the face of defeat and crushing pain resonated with Iris, and her heart skipped a beat, startling her. But instead of addressing the new sensation she had just encountered, she prioritized tending to Daedalus's wounds first as he slowly passed out.

Freya arrived with bandages and a whole suitcase full of medical supplies, much to Iris's confusion.

"He ends up like this a lot," stated Freya calmly. "Always pushing himself too hard. So, I tend to keep this nearby for such occasions."

"Is that healthy?"

"No, but it's not like you're any different."

Iris paused for a moment and touched the edges of her bangs. In the past, her hair had been a beautiful hue of pink like her mother's, but her desire to be stronger, to bring pride to the Electra family again after generations of disgrace, had pushed her to exceed her limits time and time again. This ultimately resulted in her hair turning completely white, similar to how Daedalus's was becoming. Although in her case, it settled on silver, as she colored her hair with her Luvis energy. But Iris didn't know how Freya could know that, since her hair had been silver ever since she was a young teenager.

"I suppose you're right. I guess that's also part of his charm."

"It is."

Freya gently picked up Daedalus's arm and started treating it by applying a disinfectant to his wounds.

Meanwhile, Iris prepared the bandages with a special cream with practiced precision, as she took a moment to remember how many times she'd put herself in a similar state as Daedalus in the past.

"When he wakes up, tell him I'll approve his request to formally join the RAL," said Alice, walking up to the trio with Frederika right behind her. "He gave me a fantastic display of not just his skills but his guts and raw willpower. He should be interesting to watch grow within the league."

"He's more impressive than I originally pegged him for," admitted Frederika. "I suppose it's worth seeing how the league will help mold him. Although, he will need to toughen up more. I doubt he'll get used to ending up like this."

"He already is." Freya sighed.

"Oh…well. Let's see how he lasts then."

Frederika shrugged, and Alice gave the two girls a final wave before heading toward the exit.

"Make sure to properly care for him," she called back. "Bye-bye!"

The two left, and Iris and Freya continued working on Daedalus's arm with nearly surgical precision and care. After a brief discussion, they decided to take him to the dorm to recover rather than the hospital.

There, Daedalus spent the better part of a day recovering. Due to his innate healing factor as a Radiant, his wounds disappeared before he woke up, leaving him looking exactly the same, except for the white in his hair that had spread slightly farther.

CHAPTER 12

Old and New

Following his acceptance into the RAL, Daedalus found himself much more excited about the development than he'd expected. Similarly, Freya and Iris both wanted to congratulate and celebrate him getting accepted. Although, they couldn't agree about how to do so.

Iris was also feeling somewhat guilty about having hurt him, but after a lot of reassurance, she started getting over it. Still, it didn't stop her from offering Daedalus various gifts as tokens of apology.

Eventually, they all decided to just go shopping and spend a day outside of the school to celebrate. This led them to the Delta Mall, which was located in the city of Braveheart, a large metroplex connected directly to the Regulus University campus. The campus was large enough to be its own city, and it directly influenced

Braveheart to become a bustling metropolis full of malls, shops, and places of entertainment.

Both Freya and Iris resolved themselves to get Daedalus something worthwhile, even though he insisted that their sentiments were enough. In Freya's case, she wanted to get him something that might help with his training. In Iris's, she wanted to get something that would help him relax.

"How about these Hyper-durex weights?" said Freya. "The whole set is only two-thousand Luvos."

"Don't you think that's a bit expensive?" asked Daedalus, cringing at the price tag.

"No."

"What? Iris, don't you think two-thousand Luvos is too much for a gift?"

"Hm, Stryker is being too cheap, is what I think," replied Iris, who was wearing a pink wig and blue color contacts to hide her identity. Freya didn't have on any sort of disguise, since it seemed no one recognized her when she wasn't in her "golden" form.

"What? Are you two made of money?" asked Daedalus.

"Somewhat, I suppose."

"Yes."

Both Freya and Iris casually answered without missing a beat.

Due to their positions in the league, it would be no exaggeration to say that money was the least of their worries. With the royalties made from their visage in merchandise, they could've most likely paid countless tuitions to Regulus, but for the most part, neither of them really cared to spend much money on themselves or otherwise. Unfortunately, this gave them a bad perception of the value of money.

This was somewhat understandable for Iris, since she was the daughter of the head of the Electra family, who never hurt for money on any day. But for Freya, this made little sense. Although, what Daedalus didn't know was that she had only recently developed the same skewed perception as Iris due to the sheer amount of money she had accrued. This, when combined with how little she generally cared about most things, led to her having no sense of proper money management. Not that it really mattered. She spent so little money and made so much that it would've been almost impossible for her to go broke.

"I think Daedalus would like these." Iris smiled, holding up a neck massaging machine. "His back will most likely be sore. Perhaps the chair, too? Might as well cover his whole body. What do you think, Stryker?"

"Hm, I prefer using a wooden roller. What do you think, Daedalus?"

"It's too expensive!" yelled Daedalus, nearly fainting from the price tag—six-thousand Luvos. "Do you know how much rent you could pay with this much money?"

Iris and Freya looked at each other before answering at the same time.

"No."

"I'm surrounded by rich women." He groaned. "With no sense of the value of money."

Daedalus walked over to the cheaper side of the table, where Iris was looking at products, and picked up a small hand massaging apparatus.

"How about this instead? It's only ten Luvos."

"No. That doesn't even look well made. You would expect me to buy something that isn't of quality?" Iris frowned. "That's mildly insulting."

"It's a bit rude," agreed Freya.

There wasn't anything that could be done in the current situation, so Daedalus simply sighed and let the two do whatever they wanted. Which ended up being the worst possible thing he could have done. A few minutes later, they walked out of the shop with a group of employees carting loads of stuff.

"What the hell? Return all of that!" yelled Daedalus. "Did you buy the whole store?"

"No…"

"I doubt it. Probably a good eighty percent left."

Among the goods the two had bought, Daedalus could see massage chairs, machines, weights, and all sorts of exercise or relaxation-related goods. There was no way all of it would fit inside their dorm, which begged the question of where they thought all that stuff was going to be stored.

"So…we got a bit carried away," said Iris, awkwardly. "Turned into a bit of a competition, and we just realized that there is no realistic place for you to put any of these."

"You don't think?"

"Right…so, I'm probably just going to put the stuff I bought in storage somewhere."

"Why not just return it?"

"Principle," answered Iris and Freya.

"Right…"

"Take my stuff into storage too, Electra," said Freya, who was eyeing the stuff she'd bought with a disinterested look.

"If that is what you want, just try to claim it or do something with it in a timely manner," said Iris. "Perhaps donate it to the needy. I'm sure the needy need some relaxation in their lives."

"I'll think about it after Daedalus chooses his gift. How about you?"

"I had the same idea."

Iris let out a soft sniff as she glared at Freya, who returned her look. The two seemed like they were still at odds with each other, but by now, Daedalus had gotten used to them bickering. It was a strange dynamic to him, though, since at times they were capable of cooperation, but in other situations, the two just couldn't see eye to eye.

"So, what's next?" asked Daedalus, remembering that this store in the mall was just their first stop. Worry entered his mind as he thought about what else they were going to buy.

"Summer is coming along. I need to get a new swimsuit," said Freya.

"Swimsuit? I thought you didn't go out, Stryker?"

"I'm making an exception this year."

"Then I'll join you. While I don't usually purchase swimwear from these sorts of locations, I think experiencing different things is good for one's mind. Do you have a preference, Daedalus?"

"Hm...I'm usually pretty neutral. Since different people make different swimsuits look good. You know? Why do you ask?"

"So you can pick mine out for me." Iris smiled.

"Are you sure? I feel like I have a crappy sense of style. I literally wear the same style every day."

Daedalus showed off his outfit of jeans and a T-shirt with a wave of his hand. But Iris didn't seem to care about how bland his fashion sense was, and insisted on him choosing her swimsuit. This led to Freya wanting the same treatment. Only, her excuse was that she wanted a "unique change of pace" that she felt she wasn't capable of achieving on her own.

"Before that, though, I need to head to the little Radiants' room. Do you know where that is?" said Daedalus.

"Hm...probably on the other side of the mall."

"Yup."

"Always the other side." Daedalus groaned. "I'll meet up with you two at the shop. You're going to Mermaids Lullaby, right?"

"That's correct. I suppose I'll try out a few while I wait. Get accustomed to the general feel. I'm hoping they have something of acceptable quality."

Freya rolled her eyes. "It's a swimsuit. Not battle regalia, Electra."

"Yes, well, we wouldn't want any accidents happening, now would we, Stryker? I happen to need strong support due to my...bountiful assets. If the fabric is too weak, it'll break."

"Yes, I know. I have the same problem."

The two were at it again, and Daedalus let out a sigh before starting his long jog to the other side of the mall. In the middle, he found a map, and part of him hoped that there would be another, closer restroom, but all he learned was that the two were located opposite of each other, on different floors.

I hate architecture.

On the verge of exploding, Daedalus managed to make it to the bathroom just in time. With a sigh of relief, he washed his hands after finishing his business. Now, all that was left was the annoyingly long trek to the swimsuit shop.

"Excuse me, young man."

Daedalus stopped as an elderly man's voice called out to him. He turned around but didn't spot anyone among the bustling streams of people who seemed to have been talking to him. Then, when he turned back around, he found himself face to face with a tall, elderly man in a black suit.

"Hello," said the man, with a gravelly voice.

"Hi?"

The man's eyes were closed, and he clutched a cane with an owl engraved on the top. Everything about him read as a gentleman, perhaps even a successful businessman, but Daedalus found himself instinctually weary of him. He didn't know why.

At first, he assumed it was because of the man's Luvis energy, but Daedalus quickly noticed how nearly nonexistent it was within the man. Like any other elderly Radiant, his body simply no longer produced much Luvis, which left him functionally as a normal human. But that information did little to answer why Daedalus felt so much foreboding by being near him.

"I'm looking for a certain store," said the man, "and I seem to have gotten lost."

"Ah. Yeah, it can happen. This is my first time here, so I don't know how much I can help you, but I know where to find a map."

"Oh, wonderful. Please, lead the way."

There was a certain firmness in the man's steps. A strange authority in his gait that didn't match up with the visage of an elderly person. At the same time, he had a surprisingly calming, disarming air about him.

"My name is Ray, by the way."

"Daedalus. Nice to meet you."

"Likewise."

Their meeting was short and some would even say pointless, but after locating his destination and leaving, Ray's presence still left a chilling impression on Daedalus. He hadn't experienced anything like it before. What he didn't notice was that the cause of his unease wasn't Ray himself, but his shadow that lagged behind him ever so slightly. It tipped a fedora that Ray himself wasn't wearing.

Seems like a nice guy. I wonder who he's looking for. Maybe his granddaughter?

Daedalus watched Ray enter the store. A loud, excited voice greeted him. It was a heartwarming moment, but Daedalus didn't have time to stay and watch. Iris and Freya were waiting for him.

Upon reaching the swimwear shop, Daedalus went inside and started looking around. The place seemed normal, calm, quiet, and suspiciously lacking in either Iris or Freya. Both of whom he would have easily noticed inside the store due to their heights.

Where'd they go? Are they changing?

The inside of the store was much more colorful than the rest of the white mall. Summer-related decorations were strewn about the place, and a large shark skull hung over the cashier's desk. There were also racks upon racks of different women's swimsuits of various styles. From modest swimwear to pieces of string that were tied over a metal frame, Daedalus was sure anyone could find anything they were looking for in the store. Except for men, who only had a small corner with various trunks.

"This one has hibiscuses on it. Nice. Although, these navy-blue ones speak to me too."

Despite the small selection, Daedalus found himself sufficiently entertained by the different trunks and their simplistic designs. So much so that he forgot that he was looking for Freya and Iris. At least, until he heard someone clear their throat behind him.

"Having fun, Daedalus?" Iris gave him a small smile as she looked over his shoulder at the red trunks with pink hearts in his hands. "A bit tacky, but you could make it work. Especially if there is a certain message you are trying to get across."

"You think so?"

"I do. More importantly, though, Freya is waiting for us in the changing rooms. She accurately surmised that you would get distracted upon entering and asked me to come look for you."

"Why didn't she come get me herself?"

"She's having a bit of trouble with her chosen suit. It appears her sizes don't agree very well with it. So, she is looking for a larger size that still compliments her figure."

"And you?"

"Of course, I managed to find a suitable outfit. Her choice of style is the root of the issue that I've learned to avoid."

"So, you went with a bikini and Freya probably went for a one-piece?"

"Oh! You know me so well already. How flattering. That's correct on both fronts."

Freya was always one to wear things with efficiency and function over appearance. That's what made her battle regalia as Gold Prominence so weird for Daedalus to see her in. It had tons of needless, dangling parts, but he was certain that the aesthetics were forced on her by the school to make sure she had an image befitting a RAL Champion.

"Anyways, follow me," said Iris. "Let's head to the changing rooms so that the judging may begin."

"Judging?"

"I'm pretty sure we mentioned you were going to help us choose, no?"

"Right…"

Iris pulled Daedalus along with a sly smile. Once they were in front of the row of tall, rectangular changing stalls, she positioned him in between two specific ones.

"Wait here. When I say I'm ready, I'll tell you to give us a countdown and we will come out together."

"Why not just come out as you finish changing…"

"Don't ruin the sport." Iris smiled, putting a finger up and winking.

A subtle rummaging sound was coming from the changing room next to the one Iris went into. It was like someone was having trouble organizing themselves or getting something on, which made Daedalus chuckle because he knew it was probably Freya. Then, unexpectedly, he sensed Freya's aura condense, and he could see golden energy flowing out from behind the curtain.

Wait, did she transform? Why?

"All right, Daedalus, I'm ready! Countdown when you can," called Iris.

"Um. Are you ready, Freya?"

"Yes," she called back.

"All right, Guess I'm counting down then…" Daedalus sighed. "Three…two…one…zero!"

The curtain to Iris's changing room swung open with a grace and finesse that one would expect of someone as prestigious as her. It was almost like she had specifically practiced how to open curtains quickly and elegantly in the past, but that concept was almost laughably ridiculous to Daedalus.

Freya, on the other hand, revealed herself in a much clumsier manner, but neither of those things mattered to Daedalus a moment later. His eyes almost popped out of his head as he looked at the two women in their swimsuits.

To his left, Iris was wearing a beautiful bikini that wrapped around her body magnificently, with an overall style that revealed a lot but still left enough to the imagination that it felt like a very well executed tease. The simplicity of the bikini also helped highlight the beautiful complexity of her body and the definition of her supple, well-trained muscles. Especially her abdomen.

In the face of such overwhelming beauty, anyone would've expected a competitor to be immediately washed out. Like eating a gourmet steak and then comparing it to a discount bargain meat, but Freya held up immensely well as she took a confident step out with her majestic golden hair and eyes, giving off a powerful, Amazonian impression.

Unlike Iris, and as expected by Daedalus, she had chosen to go for functionality over appearance. Because of this, Freya was wearing a uniquely designed one-piece swimsuit that highlighted her hips and curves. Even her bust was well accentuated by the tight, supportive material, which added to her intense allure.

Freya also wore a stylish jacket that gave her overall outfit a complex and unique feel.

"Well, what do you think?" asked Iris, striking a pose.

"Is it weird?" asked Freya, who noticed Iris posing and tried to do one of her own.

"Hm…I think you both look fantastic."

Daedalus stroked his chin, deep in thought. Each of his eyes was focused on either Iris or Freya. His brain tried to force itself to capture the whole scene at once, but only ended up giving him a headache. He squeezed his eyes closed and opened them again to make it go away.

"Could you both turn around?"

Iris and Freya looked at each other before switching sides.

Once again, Iris struck a practiced pose that increased how attractive she looked, and Freya did her best to manage something similar. Although, in Daedalus's opinion, she really didn't need to pose to increase her sex appeal. Neither of them did.

"Daedalus…" said Iris, her tone suspicious. "Are you actually checking how we look or are you just checking us out?"

"Uh…the first?"

A bright light exploded in front of Daedalus's eyes, and he was temporarily blinded by the sudden illumination, but rather then yell he simply smacked his lips.

"All right, that's fair. I deserved that," he said, while waiting for his vision to return.

"Admire our beauty later. Right now, what's important is picking out the optimal swimsuit," scolded Iris. "There are still many others to go through. So, don't be going slack-jawed just yet, Daedalus."

"Wait, there's more?"

"Of course, there is! You think we would just pick one and go? No! We have a whole selection for you to choose from. We are counting on you to pick the best one. Right, Freya?"

Freya nodded as she fiddled with a hoodie that had randomly appeared over her original jacket by flipping the hood on and off.

"That's a lot of pressure…"

Daedalus took a deep breath as the two went back into the changing room. A small team of attendants showed up with an assortment of swimsuits for the both of them. The realization set in that he had signed up for a long, tedious process, and it was going to leave him physically exhausted and mentally drained.

CHAPTER 13

Grand Slam

"Welcome, everyone, to the Radiant Amateur League Season Inaugural Grand Slam Tournament!"

The flamboyantly dressed announcer slammed his microphone onto the floor, where it bounced up and back into his hands as he let out an enthusiastic yell. His call echoed even without the mic, and the thousands of audience members all exploded into fervent cheering as a series of projections appeared floating in the middle of the Star Seven Arena. An impressive Radiant Arena in its own right, but one that was still dwarfed by the Grand Regulus Arena.

Each projection displayed a full-body look of one of the fighters participating in the tournament, including an intense, cross-armed Gold Prominence and a confident-looking still frame of the Lightning Empress.

"As is tradition, the season will start off with an explosive and exciting tournament featuring the best Radiants in the Amateur League and the "rookies," Radiants who have been recently admitted into the league for showing great promise and capabilities to stand toe to toe with the best right off the bat!"

The crowd's fervent cheering intensified as more projections appeared on the screen. Only this time, instead of uniformed individuals, a group of new faces appeared who were all wearing the same outfit.

Unlike their experienced predecessors, all the rookies wore the Radiant battle uniform. Which was really just black tight-fitting shorts and a shirt with colored stripes to match their university. The reason for this was because the privilege of getting your own battle regalia was something only granted to Radiants who proved themselves in battle. For many in the RAL, their first goal was to distinguish themselves enough to earn one.

"Today we have many different well-known Radiants on the battlefield. Among them, of course, we have the ever-oppressive Gold Prominence, Freya Stryker, and the Lightning Empress, Iris Electra! But we also have the Crimson Princess, Scarlett Maia, and White Winter, Penelope Taygeta!"

As the announcer called out their names, 3D projections of them re-appeared, reenacting a series of moves for everyone to cheer to. Including Daedalus, who was wearing a Gold Prominence hat and had a Gold Prominence foam finger in his right hand, along with a Lightning Empress T-shirt with matching foam finger in his left.

This made him quite the odd man out, as he sat in a VIP skybox that had been given to him courtesy of both Iris and Freya, who'd urged him to attend the great debut match. Frankly, Daedalus had hoped to be invited as one of the rookies, but at the end of the day, the VIP seats weren't that bad either.

The judgmental stares of the other people sitting there didn't make the situation any better, though. One elder woman's particularly nasty gaze made him wince.

"Excuse me. I believe my seat is right next to yours."

A calm, beautiful voice spoke from above, and Daedalus stood up to give the owner a way to their seat. Due to the rim of his hat, he couldn't really make out who they were, but he could tell they were a fairly tall person wearing some sort of qipao.

"Thank you. Those are very novel accessories you have there."

"Thanks!" responded Daedalus gleefully as he sat back down. "I got them to support my friends."

"Friends? Are you associated with those two?"

"A bit, I'd say."

"Ah, I see. That explains how you are here and why I've never seen you before."

The woman let out a thoughtful hum, but she didn't seem bothered by the news of how socially unimportant Daedalus was. The elder lady, on the other hand, started complaining loudly about security letting a "nobody" into the "prestigious VIP seats."

"I will have a talk with Alice about letting these sorts of people here. I can feel the disease creeping up on me." She scowled.

"Mhm," said the woman beside her. "And to be in our box of all places. Truly, misfortune follows us like a plague."

The two elderly women kept muttering amongst themselves while sitting behind a woman with bubble-gum pink hair. She had an emotionless expression across her face, and she either didn't react or didn't care about the two women behind her.

They all have the emblem of Electra…

The three who were seated together had pins with a series of three lightning bolts that converged into a center point. The two elderly women's pins were a platinum color, designating them as retired Radiants of prestige, but what caught Daedalus's attention was the younger woman's pin, diamond with golden accents. His eyes widened.

That's the leader of the Electra…Iris's mom.

Daedalus could definitely see the resemblance between her and Iris. They were both astonishingly beautiful, and he could even sense a similar sadness coming off the mom that he felt at times from Iris. Part of him wanted to greet her, but the words of the two elders behind her made him feel that it would be a bad idea. So, instead, he just continued being excited for the matches.

"Don't mind them. The old tend to be crusty and rude," said the woman sitting next to him, chuckling. "It's one of the benefits of getting old, I guess. Being tolerated. I sure hope I don't end up like that."

The woman crossed her legs and leaned back. Daedalus was starting to feel rude about not being able to make eye contact with her, so he lifted up the front of his hat. He caught sight of a pair of icy-blue eyes and jaw-droppingly beautiful pale blonde hair.

"Madam?" Daedalus blurted out.

"The one and only." She smiled. "You noticed much later than most people usually do. You are pretty disinterested in things such as status and prestige, aren't you? Most normal people would be trying to strike up conversations with everyone in this box right now. Trying to get an in, a lead, some ticket to wealth."

"It's not my style. If anything, I'd rather get there myself with the help of genuine friends. My name is Daedalus, by the way."

"I can tell." She laughed. "That's good. This world has placed far too much value on pointless things such as 'fame' and 'pedigree'... Daedalus, huh? I'll remember that."

"That's rich coming from a non-seven Pleiades. You seem to be enjoying your status pretty comfortably," called out one of the Electra elders. "Don't be cocky over a fluke. You will be replaced by the time the next tournament comes around."

"Always so hateful." Madam sighed. "I wonder if it's because their family can't produce a Radiant capable of even qualifying for the Grand Tournament!"

Madam smirked at the elder, who gritted her teeth and slammed her hand on the armrest. "If that Iris weren't such a disgraceful letdown, I'd be able to say something," the woman muttered.

"What's she talking about?" asked Daedalus, confused about her comment. "Isn't Iris a really great Radiant? Ranked number two?"

"Yes, but since she isn't number one, the family is bitter. Especially since she is losing to someone who isn't from one of the Seven Great Families. Not to mention, Iris isn't very mindful of Electra tradition."

"What do you mean?"

"The way she uses the Electra style is considered a bastardization by the family. A corruption and disgusting twisting of their 'proud' and 'noble' form. Or so they say. I find it pretty refreshing and perhaps even what they need to become relevant again."

"What's so different about it?"

"The Electra style is a distance-controlling fighting style. They use their electricity to create distance, keep it, and attack from afar. Iris uses a unique close-combat style where she rarely stays at long ranges. And even if she does, she tactically choses when to be far away for certain things, but most of the time she is right in her opponent's face. Apparently, the Electra think that's barbaric."

Madam shrugged and took a sip of her drink from the counter behind her. She offered the cup to Daedalus, who raised an eyebrow.

"It's apple juice," she said. "It's good."

"Uh, thanks?"

Daedalus awkwardly grabbed the cup and took a sip. He gave it back to Madam before realizing how unusually delicious the juice was.

"Tasty, right?" She smiled.

"Surprisingly so... Is that a special blend?"

"How interesting of you to notice! Yes, this is my special apple juice that I make using the apples I grow in my personal garden. It's more than just one apple, but I mixed it so that the flavors are multiplied and more impactful than normal juice."

"I was wondering about that subtle sourness. Easy to miss."

"Exactly! But it's prevalent enough to really stir up the senses. I think it'll be a huge hit with my customers as a hangover remedy."

"Honestly, it might just be. That's pretty cool."

"Thank you, I appreciate the genuine praise. I don't get it very often."

Daedalus tilted his head. "Really? You're a Pleiades. I'd think you'd get praise a lot."

"That's just people blowing smoke," Madam said with a dismissive wave of her hand. "Your praise was more from the heart. It had substance. I could see in your eye that if it tasted bad, you'd tell me."

"Probably."

Madam snickered before putting the juice back on the counter behind her. She placed her hands on her lap.

"Well, let us prepare to enjoy the tournament... Say, you wouldn't happen to have more of those interesting accessories, would you? I feel the urge to share in your delightful decorations. Rarely if ever do people come with such fun articles of clothing."

"I have these shirts, these caps, this sweatband, this jacket…"

Daedalus began flatly naming off all the extra stuff he was keeping on his person and under his seat. All of which were gifts from Freya and Iris, who had once again created a competition out of seeing whose merchandise he'd wear. This ended up just swamping him with merch he really didn't need, so having someone else to unload some of it onto was honestly a relief for him.

"Oh! I'll take these."

Within minutes, Madam had placed a baggy Lightning Empress T-shirt over her qipao, while donning a Gold Prominence headband and happi coat. While many would've expected this to destroy her graceful, proud visage, somehow, even with the hodgepodge of extra clothing, she still gave off an air of nobleness and confidence, though more playful and less intimidating.

"This is fun." She chuckled. "Let us begin the hype!"

Madam waved her foam finger wildly with a childish grin, and the lights from the arena suddenly dimmed to focus on the battlefield. As they did, powerful, high-energy music began blasting out of a series of hidden speakers, and the first pair of fighters made their way toward the middle of the field. As they walked, the crowd's enthusiasm reached a new high.

"Round one! We have a fan favorite from Ryuguin University! The Purveyor of Pain! The Titan of Torment! Also known as the Crimson Princess! Scarletttttt Maiaaaaaaaaaaaaa!"

Wearing red-themed, fantasy-style battle regalia, the woman named Scarlett reached the middle of the field. She had jet black hair that covered her eyes, and she looked oddly unimposing compared to what Daedalus was used to seeing from high-ranked Radiants. Usually, they exuded confidence and strength. Instead, Scarlett seemed shy.

This was further exemplified as the camera panned around her face. Daedalus had never seen Scarlett Maia before but had read a lot about her "fiery" fighting style and "intense" ferocity that "burned all competitors away." He twisted his mouth, feeling like he was missing something.

"Facing her is the newcomer to the RAL, hailing from Centoria University! A Radiant with great promise, a new face from a branch of the Electra family! Katie Hugar-Electra!"

The lighting shifted from Scarlett and focused on a woman with her light blue hair tied into a ponytail. Her eyes looked determined, and she walked with a sort of forced confidence. It was obvious she was nervous but doing her best not to show it.

Katie reached the middle of the battlefield, and Scarlett offered her a handshake. Yet, the gesture was left unanswered, as Katie hesitated and ultimately refused to take it with another forced look of toughness.

In response, Scarlett pulled her hair back with an orange glowing hand that caused it to stay slicked back, beautifully and neatly. This revealed her full face for the first time to Daedalus. His eyes went wide.

Hidden behind the bangs were a pair of extremely dangerous-looking, sharp red eyes. Easily the most naturally intense eyes he had ever seen in his life, they completely shifted her appearance from shy to arrogant, even though she still had the same meek smile on her lips. Her irises had a black ring around them that further strengthened her gaze and visibly unnerved Katie.

So, that's why she keeps her bangs long. It's like Freya's problem, but hers is more physical and frankly, easier to hide.

"It'd appreciate it if you didn't stare too much," said Scarlett, kindly. "It's embarrassing when my opponent looks so much. But I can't fight with my bangs in my face. I'm sorry about the inconvenience."

Katie gulped and brought her fists up. Scarlett seemed somewhat apologetic, but without saying anything, she brought one leg back before entering a stoic, almost mountain-esque stance. Her black hair then flared up for a moment as random strands suddenly burst into flames.

This provoked another round of applause and whistles from the crowd. At the same time, Daedalus and Madam both began waving their foam fingers wildly, earning multiple looks from some of the other VIPs. But neither of them cared for their opinions and instead wanted to only enjoy the tournament.

"All fighters at the ready! Match One of the Radiant Grand Slam!" yelled the announcer. "Begin!"

* * *

The sounds of the first match starting were met with noise that even Frederika could hear from outside the arena. In her left hand, she held an unlit cigarette, and in her right was a lollipop. She flicked the cigarette away and popped the candy into her mouth with a long sigh.

"It's getting easier, right?"

"Hardly. I can't even tell."

"It's better for you in the long run. Trust me! Besides, you're too young to be using stuff like that."

Alice popped up behind Frederika with a wide smile. She firmly pounded Frederika's back before turning her attention out toward the vast field that made up the outside of the Star Seven Arena. The sky was calm and the trees waved gently in the distance, but all of that only served to disarm the people keeping watch for a supposed greater threat.

"Anything?"

"'Fraid not!"

Regulus University had received a tip that there was going to be some sort of violent assault committed during the Grand Slam. All the universities had deployed their best Security Radiants to keep the area under tight lockdown, but so far, things had remained deathly quiet.

"Who do you think it is?"

"Probably the Numbers. Although, who knows. Tension has been building up amongst the Seven, so it could be related to that. Or, worst case, it's Night. We all know how much he hates the current system." Alice shrugged.

"He isn't going to do anything, though. He's too old at this point. And if it was the Seven, wouldn't you know? Aren't you the Princess of the Alcyone?"

"No...I'm the super cute, omega popular Idol Alice-Alice!"

Alice jumped up onto one foot and made a sideways peace sign. In response, Frederika pushed her over with a disgusted look on her face.

"I hate it when you do that. I don't even know why you choose to look like *that*."

"Because it's cute!" replied Alice, as she grabbed her pink twin ponytails and shook them. "You can't become a mega idol without cuteness!"

"Whatever."

The calmness and tranquility outside of the arena stretched on, undisturbed and unbothered. But everyone on guard knew better than to take any sort of tip lightly. That had happened once before and had created one of the greatest tragedies in recent history, so there was no lightheartedness among any of the people watching. Danger could strike at any moment.

Frederika sniffed. "The quietness is off-putting."

"As a performer, I do enjoy the sound of the audience cheering me on, but moments of quiet are nice too."

"Not in this situation."

The air shifted slightly as Frederika and Alice waited. The gnawing boredom threatened to lull both of them to sleep, but when a feeling of foreboding crawled up Frederika's back, she knew something was going on. Even if she wasn't seeing what that "something" was.

"I'm going to check in with everyone."

"K!" said Alice.

"This is Black Eagle performing rollcall for all squads. Respond immediately," ordered Frederika into her earpiece.

"Robin Blue, checking in. Sector A. Clear."

"Canary Red, checking in. Sector B. Clear."

"Swallow Green, checking in. Sector C. Clear."

"Black Eagle, this is Big Cheese. I'm noticing strange movement in the eastern sector," came another voice through a communicator on Frederika's wrist. She turned to Alice.

"Isn't the East being guarded by Ryguin?"

"It should be. Why?"

"Centoria's security leader just called out strange movements…" Frederika brought up the communicator and switched it to Ryguin's output frequency.

"This is Black Eagle, calling in to Thunder One. Big Cheese has reported strange movement in your vicinity. Be advised. Do you copy?"

Silence.

"Thunder One, this is Black Eagle. Do you copy?"

Nothing.

"Oh, great. Looks like we have a situation. Didn't we agree to tell each other about situations?" Frederika groaned. "Big Cheese, we have a situation. Thunder One is unresponsive. Be advised that—"

"That the enemy may attack? Yes. That is a healthy assumption to make, Reaper."

An unknown voice suddenly spoke through the communicator, and a chill raced down Frederika's spine. Alice's smile dropped off her face, and a small, serious frown replaced it.

"One thing after another. Since when do the 'three great universities' have such crappy security teams?"

Frederika turned the head of the wrist communicator, and when its screen flashed red, she slammed her hand into it. Immediately, an emergency call was sent out to every single guard in the venue. Alice produced a small stick from her dress that extended into a full microphone stand.

"I guess things will get more exciting than I thought." Frederika sighed, and then a sinister smile appeared on her lips. "Good thing I was getting bored."

She threw her hand out, and a ball of purple Luvis energy came to life in the air. Frederika crushed the orb with her hand, and the energy exploded outward before turning into a wicked-looking scythe made of pure purple Luvis, emitting a sinister hum.

"Are you going to join, President?"

"Yes, I suppose, if I must." Alice grinned, with a surprisingly sadistic look in her eyes.

* * *

"Ow. Bastard."

Frederika rubbed her forehead where an enemy attack had just landed. The blow had disoriented her slightly, but otherwise, she was unscathed due to the thick personal Luvis barrier around her. It was strong enough to deflect all projectiles, and even Luvis weapons had trouble cracking it. But that didn't mean she wouldn't occasionally feel the blows from significant hits.

"Have you gotten a bit rusty, Rika?" asked Alice, who was rapidly spinning her mic stand in different directions to deflect incoming projectiles. "If you'd like to take a moment to sit down and rest, I could arrange that for you."

"I'm fine."

Following the disrupted communications from both the Ryuguin and Centoria University security teams, Frederika had pulled all available personal outside of the arena to reinforce the entrances, so no one could sneak in amidst the fighting, and to help repel the attacks. Even though no one had confirmed a visual yet, everyone was on edge and wary to see what exactly had taken out two professional defense forces so quickly and quietly.

Then, like shadows, multiple armed people appeared across the fields, including assassins who attempted to take out Frederika and Alice before the fighting could begin. But, unfortunately for the attackers, whatever blade or method they tried would never work against someone who was infinitely better at being a killer than they ever could be.

"Status report on the gates?" asked Frederika, who sidestepped an attack before cutting the assassin in half with her scythe.

"Gate A is holding. Situation is under control."

"Gate B is under heavy assault, but we are holding."

"Gate C is sustaining heavy casualties…we can hold."

"That's what I like to hear," said Frederika, as a Luvis arrow whistled toward her. "Me and the President are going to start mopping up this mess. I was hoping to see something interesting, but this is as boring as anything else."

The arrow snapped like a twig as it hit Frederika's barrier. Her words aside, a part of her was suspicious about how the other two guard details could have fallen to such weak assailants. In spite of the fact they were part of rival schools, the guards for Ryuguin and Centoria weren't slouches or pushovers. A good chunk of them were high-ranking Radiants from the Professional League.

"Alice, we should weed them out with extreme prejudice…but—"

"But be mindful. Yes. They seem to be hiding some sort of trick. I can't imagine the guards losing to people like this without a word."

The air buzzed wildly around the two without warning, and it felt as though the air was sucked in from behind them. Both Frederik and Alice stumbled forward from the suction. They looked up to see a powerful ball of red Luvis energy hovering in the air.

"Uh."

"That looks fun."

The orb pulsed once, ripping at the landscape and burning it away before shooting out a thick laser aimed at both of them. In response, Frederika took a step back, and Alice "took the stage" with a twirl of her stand and a cute pose.

"I guess it's time for my performance!" she called out. "Let's go!"

Alice did a well-practiced forward triple step, then threw her hand up and with a loud, melodic, beautiful "la," she generated a soundwave that crashed into the laser. Immediately stopping it in its tracks before forcefully dispersing it.

A shockwave exploded outward as the attack was destroyed, and Alice did a final pose before turning back toward Frederika.

"That was just a warm-up. It's time for the Idol of the Professional League to start a concert. Don't you think?"

Out of the ground, multiple Radiants clad in full-body black clothing popped out. A singular shadow produced them, and they aimed to strike down Alice, who let out a cute "wow" as she put her hands up. With a small tap of her foot, a soundwave exploded out of the floor and shattered the bones of every assailant. The damage ignored Frederika, though, despite her being in the effective range.

"They don't even have Luvis barriers strong enough to defend against that?" Alice sighed. "Frederika…"

"Yes?"

"Take a team and sweep the inside of the building. I just heard a noise that shouldn't be there in the eastern wing."

"The VIPs?"

"I'm sure they can handle themselves, but I know the Electra elders are there, and they always complain about something. I don't want to give them more reasons than normal."

"All right."

A large Luvis blade rushed at Alice, who blocked it with the back of her microphone stand.

"As for the rest of you…"

Alice pushed the blade away with enough force that there was an audible crack from the bones in the attackers' arms. Then, she spun her stand and, like a bat, swung it into the attacker as they fell back, sending them flying far into the distance with a final wet *crack*.

"Prepare to witness the grandest performance you will ever experience!"

CHAPTER 14

Pleione

The match inside the stadium started off with an exciting bang as Katie unleashed a torrent of lightning at Scarlett. It seemed to do little to deter Maia, who used a wall of beautifully orange fire to tank most of the attacks. At the same time, though, Maia was having a hard time finding a chance to get close to Katie.

"See, that is how an Electra fights." One of the elders smiled. "From a distance, wearing out your opponent and then landing the killing strike. I like her. She has potential."

"She is the result of that one man we married into the family."

"Ah! Yes, I remember those days. I was at the end of my prime. It was certain he would have a notable Radiant in his lineage when mixed with ours. Isn't that right, Miss Luna?"

The two elders talked happily amongst themselves, obviously glad at the performance of Katie. Yet, Iris's mother, whom Daedalus gathered was named Luna, didn't seem terribly impressed or upset. In fact, she continued to have a blank, emotionless look on her face. The only hint that she was actually alive was the occasional movement of her eyes in Daedalus's direction.

"Yes, she is doing well," said Luna. "Perhaps enough to be promoted to a higher house."

"Perhaps. I have high hopes for her."

Luna let out a soft breath and crossed her legs. It was astonishing to Daedalus just how much of a similar air Iris had to her. Despite the fact her mother had pink hair and matching pink eyes, they both definitely appeared to be from the same lineage. Moreover, the way she sat there was a lot like how Iris would often sit when deep in thought or processing information.

I guess Iris got most of her mannerisms from her mom. Makes sense.

Daedalus returned his attention to the battle as Katie took a powerful blow to the stomach that sent a burst of fire outward. She let out a scream, flying multiple feet until Scarlett caught her in a torrent of fire.

Standing in the same spot, Scarlett began doing a series of kicks that each let out a crescent of fire at rapid speeds. Each one smacked into Katie with enough force to let out a *boom*, and kept her airborne as they turned in midair to lock her in place.

"It seems the Electra style is outdated. Even the close-range Maia have learned to adopt long-range tactics," said Madam, casually. "What do you think, Daedalus?"

"A balance needs to be met, or else you will have an easily abusable, glaring weakness. Of course, I say that as someone who doesn't care much for traditions." He grinned. "On the other hand, I also do know that if someone is good enough in a specialty, they can compensate for their specialty's weakness with enough training. Although, that's typically not very common."

"Well said."

There was a dull thud as Katie hit the floor, but despite the damage she had taken, she got back up to her feet to the cheers of the audience. Her eyes burned with a determination that Daedalus sympathized with, and she let out a loud yell as more electricity arced off her body.

"You don't need to push yourself so hard," said Scarlett, with a worried look. "This is just an exhibition tournament. You're going to actually hurt yourself before the real series starts. No one expects you to win."

"I expect myself to win! I need to do it for the Electra!" she yelled.

The electricity's intensity grew, and it seemed to be starting to damage Katie herself. But without paying any heed to that or Scarlett's warnings, she resumed unleashing a vicious, powerful barrage of attacks.

One in particular ricocheted off the protective barrier and caught Scarlett in the back. The shock came as a surprise to her, and she was soon struck with her guard down multiple times. The barrage kicked up copious amounts of dust into the air.

"That one hurt...ow."

Scarlett scattered the dust in the air with a stomp of her foot. She looked a bit worse for wear than before, but otherwise was fine. She quickly beat back her irritation with a deep breath.

In the same moment, Katie conjured up more electricity into another fantastic, but somewhat repetitive, display. But before she could unleash her attack, Scarlett exploded forward and let loose a singular kick to the side of Katie's face.

"The Crimson Princess is keeping things simple." Madam sighed. "For the sake of the show and to not hurt the new one's pride. A mark of good sportsmanship but...boring."

"Huh? Have your eyes gone bad? It's obvious that our Electra is keeping her on the edge of her toes. Those few setbacks are simply a difference in experience!" cried one of the elders.

"Your pride and desire to be strong blinds you. Right, Daedalus?"

Daedalus let out a soft, "Hm?" while chewing on a piece of pizza that he had taken from the still mostly full buffet in the skybox. Sauce was splattered on his face, and cheese dribbled from his mouth. He had been caught in a very unflattering position. He didn't know why Madam was asking him, though.

"Um," he started, rapidly cleaning his face. "I can't say I'm experienced enough to comment on how big the power gap is between those two, but I feel like Scarlett isn't showing her full strength. It could be because Katie isn't letting her, or maybe…another reason."

Madam chuckled softly, but she suddenly tensed up, along with every other person in the skybox.

"What the hell—"

An explosion ripped through the arena, and the shockwave shook the skybox violently.

"What's going on!? Is this an attack? Where is security?"

As if on cue, Frederika crashed through the door, landed on her back, and flipped over as her momentum carried her out of the skybox and onto the floor seats below. In her wake, a noxious purple gas spilled into the room, and immediately, everyone covered their noses.

"Devil's Breath!" yelled Madam.

Everyone in the skybox sprang to their feet, including Daedalus. Luna created a series of seals in the air that let out a beautiful pink light, which hindered the gas from moving forward. Yet despite the hinderance, it didn't take long for Daedalus to tell that the noxious purple fog was still advancing forward. His heart raced with panic.

What the hell is Devil's breath doing here!? A Class-S Anti-Radiant neurotoxin shouldn't have made it past security!

A series of sirens began blaring out from the arena speakers, signaling the need for everyone to evacuate, and immediately putting an end to the fight. Multiple officials rushed onto the battlefield to escort Katie and Scarlett to a safe place, as others began trying to manage the flow of people toward the exit. Their escape paths started getting cut off as more Devil's Breath exploded out of the hallways and through the doors.

"How tedious."

A calm, cool, and mature voice rang out from the fog in the skybox, and the visage of a young man in a suit appeared out of the dense toxic gas. Over his face, he wore a jester mask that had two large stars for eyes with an off-putting smile made out of seven smaller stars.

"Of all the people to be in this box, it would be Luna Electra." He made a *tsk* sound. "One of the very few Radiants capable of naturally nullifying Devil's Breath with her pesky healing-trait Luvis."

"Who are you?" demanded one of the elders, whose hand crackled to life with lightning.

"Hm. That's a good question. You see, I used to find myself pondering that very thing... It took a while, but ultimately, the answer is why I'm here now! Although, I suppose you weren't being so philosophical. My name is Andres. Andres Pleione. Ring a bell?"

Everyone looked around without a clue who he was.

"Of course not." Andres chuckled. "I doubt anyone here would know about the Grand Radiant Houses."

"Grand Radiant Houses?" repeated Daedalus, his brow furrowed.

"Yes! The true rulers of this world. The ones who dominated all and managed the people globally with the help of their seven loyal servant houses."

"Enough with your fantasies and conspiracies!" shouted one of the Electra elders.

She threw her hand out, and the air vibrated with the force of the electricity that shot out of her hand. Andre let out a scoff before casually plucking it out of the air. With a small twirl, he redirected the lightning right back at the elder with an even stronger force, sending her flying out of the skybox.

The boom from the contact was loud enough to cause ringing in Daedalus's ears. He could clearly see the elder was either unconscious or dead from that singular attack, as she landed on the battlefield with a thud.

"What a rude servant," said Andres, shaking his head and dusting his hand off. "Hopefully she learns her lesson. Anyways, I'd recommend everyone else not try to attack, unless you wish to suffer a similar fate. All right? Great! More to the point…if you all don't truly know who I am, then I suppose I should give you all a history lesson."

Andres looked around and snatched a piece of pizza and a glass of wine. He walked around the skybox as if he were a longtime friend crashing another close friend's party. His eyes, walk, and posture held not a care in the world. It was like the Radiants in the room were nothing to him, despite them being some of the strongest in existence.

"Long ago," he started, "there were the Grand Houses. The proud Pleione and the righteous Atlas families. They brought about the Great Radiant Revolution as the first to harness Luvis. They led the people to an era of great peace. But I like giving credit where credit is due. Those two families couldn't have made it happen without their loyal subjects. Specifically, a certain seven vassal houses."

A short pause followed as Andres took a sip of wine. He spent another moment pondering some unknown thought, and then he let out a long sigh. Daedalus glanced at Madam, wondering what she thought about this. She was watching Andres intently, her eyes sharp.

"Well, I suppose you all are smart enough to know where I'm going with this," Andres continued. "The point is, I came with a goal in mind, but since Luna Electra is here, I now have two objectives. The first is to ask Luna if she is willing to reaffirm her vassal families' vow of loyalty to the Pleiones. To serve us eternally and without question. I am not my predecessors, so I have no hate for you traitors who killed most of us off; rather, I simply want what I am owed."

"Even if what you said was true, I'd refuse," said Luna, her hand rising with a pinkish hue. "The Electra bow to no one."

Andres snorted. "That's the biggest joke I've heard all day. Everyone knows the Electra are the biggest laughingstock of the seven vassals."

"Quit calling us vassals. We are the Seven Great Families! We will have respect."

"Uh huh. Sure. Tell me, why do you think this world is in such chaos? All this war. All this strife? It's because it's controlled by people who have grown too big for their shoes. The true leaders—the ones born to lead, who created a paradise for humanity—were destroyed! Removed by the greed and jealousy of you seven servants who forgot their place. Now, because of that, unfit stooges rule this planet, and it shows."

Andres threw his empty glass against a wall, and an unusually fearsome aura came to life around him. But most threatening of all, the Devil's Breath mixed and swirled around him with his Luvis Energy.

W—How is Luvis mixing with Devil's Breath? What kind of abomination is he?

No one except Daedalus could see how Andres's Luvis was mixing with the Devil's Breath; instead, to everyone else, it simply looked like the smog was wrapping itself around him like a corrupting, corrosive boa.

"You seven idiot families disrupted peace because you insisted on being 'the best.' You removed the true rulers, and I will have that crown returned one way or another!" he yelled. "Which brings me to my second objective...Madam."

Her eyebrows rose. "Me?"

"Yes. I know of your distaste for the current system. Join us. Help us restore the world to what it should be, and I will gladly allow you a position as one of the new vassal families. I would even consider making you my wife. A wife of Pleione! That used to be the greatest honor one could hope to achieve in life."

Madam looked Andres over as he extended his hand to her, but she simply shook her head.

"I'm afraid I'll have to turn down your offer."

Andres frowned and let his hand drop. "I see. That is unfortunate. It would have made my life much easier to have another Pleiades in my corner. But I will not be so cliché as to try and force your hand. The Pleiones value freedom and intellect. Eventually, I hope you will come to see who is in the right and who is in the wrong."

"Then you'll leave peacefully?" asked Madam.

There was a tense pause. Colors burst to life around Daedalus as all the Radiants prepared to attack Andres, who hadn't yet given an answer. None of them planned to give him the full time he needed to come to a decision, though, and all at once, everyone except Daedalus, Madam, and Luna unloaded on the singular man.

"A true sign of stupidity."

Daedalus's eyes went wide as he saw something that no one else could. As everyone's attacks reached Andres, every single one evaporated back into Luvis energy, which was promptly absorbed by Andre's hand. It gave the illusion of him deflecting the attacks or smacking them away, but in reality, his Luvis aura was growing stronger with each absorbed attack.

"The Pleiones are masters of Luvis manipulation," said Andres, chuckling. "We created the concept, after all. To think that anything Luvis could hurt me is laughable."

"Then, how about this!"

Another Radiant ran forward with a powerful kick. Andre dodged it with ease before letting loose a fearsome three-hit combo that sent her body careening violently through the wall and into a heavy patch of Devil's Breath. Not even a second passed before she began screaming as the toxin did its work, slowly killing her.

"Angel's Cry!"

An angelic silhouette roared to life behind Luna, and a powerful burst of pink Luvis shot at the dying Radiant. Andres watched the Luvis fly with disinterest and shrugged.

"I'll allow it."

The energy hit the suffering woman, and immediately, the Devil's Breath dispersed. Her cries dulled as her pain eased. She then gained a gentle green glow as she fell unconscious.

"Even to us, the capability to heal with Luvis is sought after," said Andes. "I would greatly hate to have to...terminate you, Luna Electra."

"We aren't joining you. I suggest you leave before you get hurt," said Luna firmly. "You have no chance of defeating all of us here, with or without Devil's Breath."

"That is an interesting theory you propose... I would prefer not to have to test it, but I suppose I have no choice. Although, I will let Madam live as promised. I have faith she will come around after this."

Andres pulled on a pair of gloves that complemented his suit. Daedalus swallowed hard, his heart pounding. He had a bad feeling about this. He hoped Freya and Iris were somewhere far away, somewhere safe.

"So...who's first?" said Andres.

CHAPTER 15

The Armament Queen

The evacuated building served as a perfect location for Andres to eliminate multiple Radiants. After all, it was an easy task for him to force them all out onto the field as he manipulated the gas. And once they were there, there was nowhere left to run and nowhere to escape, as a large wall of Devil's Breath formed an impenetrable barrier.

"Coward." Luna snarled. "You would use—"

"I do hope you aren't about to say something as idiotic like, 'You are being unfair relying on the Devils Breath.' Who in their right mind would not use every resource at their disposal to defeat their enemies? Besides, if you haven't noticed, I've left the whole battleground itself untouched."

"You plan on attempting to execute us yourself then?" asked Luna.

"Correct. To prove a point. Though, that one there seems to just be unlucky," said Andres, pointing at Daedalus. "I sense no real power from him. What a shame that you were rewarded with such a fine seat to watch a fantastic event, boy, only to end up in this situation. It's so tragic. I may let you live if you don't interfere. Maybe…probably not. But who knows, right?"

Daedalus kept his face expressionless, not wanting to show how scared he was.

Andres flexed his fingers and took a deep breath as he examined his left hand. He seemed oddly preoccupied with it as he meticulously scanned the glove, until he brought his attention back to the group. For a moment, Daedalus could see a gleeful eye behind the mask, a clear sign that Andres was enjoying tormenting them.

"So, one at a time or all at once? Up to you."

"Allow me to volunteer. Alone."

Madam stepped forward. All the merchandise on her body burned away from her intense Luvis. Andres let out a sharp clicking sound when the gently smiling Pleiades stood squarely in front of him.

"Madam, I don't want to hurt you. You will be left unscathed. I only want to enjoy executing the rest of them."

"Regardless, I will be your opponent. Let us see if you are strong enough to overcome a Pleiades. That

would definitely send a strong message. Especially if it's me."

"Very well. I suppose that is another good use of you. Yet, ultimately, a waste. I will try not to kill you, but I can't make promises. I have a problem holding back."

Daedalus and the rest of the Radiants backed away at Madam's signal to give her space. Then, Luna conjured up a large barrier to protect them from the upcoming destruction.

The whole group had decided to honor Madam's wishes to fight alone, and that was probably due to their faith that she could easily beat Andres. At the same time, the remaining Electra elder hurried to the back of the group to pick up her fallen comrade from before. Daedalus had honestly forgotten about her. Surprisingly, she was still alive, and with Luna's healing, he had no doubt she'd eventually recover.

"Whenever you're ready," said Andres, with a small bow.

Give him hell, Madam, thought Daedalus.

* * *

Madam scanned the battlefield around her. She couldn't see any sort of traps or sense something amiss aside from the billowing entrapment of Devil's Breath. The gas was staying oddly fixed in place, though. At the very least, she was certain Andres didn't have any reinforcements, but she did worry about what would happen to the gas once she defeated him.

If his power is keeping it in place, once it's gone…it'll all fall down…

"If you're worried about the gas, it'll dissipate harmlessly if you defeat me," said Andres, as if reading her mind.

"Is that a promise?"

"More like a fact. Maintaining it requires my power, after all. So, technically, you are getting a handicap."

"How arrogant of you to think that a Pleiades needs a handicap." She smirked as she made her way toward the center of the field where Andres was waiting.

Madam swung her arm out. She chose to believe Andres's words due to his arrogance. He seemed too proud of a human to lie about his own weakness. And even if he was lying, it wasn't like she could make any progress on a solution that didn't require defeating him first.

"Dawnbreaker!"

The air crackled, and beautiful green Luvis energy roared to life around Madam. It created a bright, blinding light, and out of the corner of her vision, she noticed Daedalus's eyes widening as an enormous double-barreled mech took form out of the energy.

"Oh. That must be your famous full ballistic mech. Very impressive." Andres clapped.

The large robot stood at least fifty feet tall, easily taller than a two-story house, and was primed on four legs with an edgy, futuristic design. It was also armed with five extremely large barrels that all pointed at Andres.

"It's every bit as amazing up close as—"

BOOM

Dawnbreaker opened fire on Andres as he was in the middle of speaking, unleashing an intense level of destruction. The raw heat of the explosions stretched behind Luna's Luvis barrier, making Daedalus and the others stumble back, wincing.

The barrage continued for multiple seconds, until one of the mech's legs suddenly exploded and it collapsed, much to Madam's shock.

Impossible! Dawnbreaker's defenses are enough to survive against even the other Pleiades' strongest attacks.

Like an aluminum can being crushed under someone's hand, Dawnbreaker continued crumpling until it shattered into multiple pieces of Luvis that sparkled out of existence.

"I told you. Luvis won't work on me."

Out of the dust of the constant barrage, Andres stomped his foot to blow away all the debris surrounding him, then casually dusted off his blazer. There didn't seem to be a single scratch on him, although the very edge of his mask had taken some damage; part of it had chipped off.

"So, you can manipulate Luvis at a distance," said Madam.

"Correct. I can also see Luvis. Even before what you do takes form, I have a pretty good idea of what it's going to do. Isn't that fun?"

"Seeing Luvis? What an outlandish lie. Not even our most advanced technologies can visualize Luvis energy. It can only detect it at best, which is a basic skill that any trained Radiant can learn."

"That's just another difference between you and me. It makes sense that members of the family that ushered in Luvis would be able to see it, no? It's a right of true nobility and a good mark of who the fakers are."

Madam flicked her hands out, and two handguns appeared in her palms. Spinning them quickly, she brought them up and shot an endless barrage of high-speed bullets at Andres, who dodged them with the grace of a ballroom dancer.

The handguns proving ineffective, Madam slammed the two of them together into a one-handed grenade launcher and lobbed a Luvis-grenade at Andres. It exploded with an intensity one could never hope to achieve with an actual hand explosive.

"What a well-earned nickname. Armament Queen. Show me what else you can do! Show me your arsenal!"

Andres jumped to the side with his hands in his pockets. He was easily riding the shockwaves of each attack, and his lack of intention to fight back made Madam increasingly wary of what he had in store. She was also taking the opportunity to gauge his capabilities.

Surviving and destroying Dawnbreaker means he really can disrupt Luvis. At a long distance, no less. He is dodging the bullets, which means that his ability might be limited by his speed of reflex, and he isn't using it on the grenades. Why?

The launcher shifted into a minigun, and Madam unleashed a hailstorm of bullets against Andres, who started moving faster to stay out of the bullets' reach. Then he flickered out of sight. A second later, Madam's minigun was launched into the air as he kicked it up. Andre then brought out his palm to attack Madam directly.

"Long distance threat, but easy to contend with in close range."

"Is that what you think?"

A fiendish smile spread on Madam's lips, and in a move that was only made possible due to her long legs, she cracked her heel down onto the back of Andre's neck before expertly twisting him around and kicking him away with the sound of a powerful gunshot. On Madam's heel, a partial handgun had taken form as part of her shoe.

Andres flew back, his blood splattering across the floor, until he tumbled to a stop. The only sound he could make was, "Tch," as he caught his breath.

"You really think I would use all of my abilities while participating in public tournaments? Of course, I keep a few things hidden away." Madam smirked. "Otherwise, it would be too easy to find my weaknesses and kill me, don't you think?"

Andres held his shoulder where the bullet had pierced through. He let out a huff as the air around him became infinitely more serious. She sensed he was quite angry with her

* * *

For Daedalus, Andres's Aura exploded with malicious, murderous intent. *That can't be good*, he thought.

"Enough of this," snapped Andres.

Once again, Andre was lost to Daedalus's vision, but a moment later, he and Madam reappeared over different parts of the battlefield as their blows connected. It seemed that Madam's fighting style revolved around kicking, similar to Daedalus's new fighting style, but her attacks were all combined with multiple different guns.

Every kick included a shot that came from her heel or a nearby floating armament. This forced Andres to keep tabs on not just her but where she was placing her weapons in the high-speed battle. And that quickly started to overwhelm him, as it became too much to keep track off.

Whenever Madam blocked, a gunshot followed from one of the two handguns tight in her hands. But if Andres spent too much time thinking about anything, the Pleiades quickly took advantage of that millisecond pause to land powerful blows. And his ability to destroy the Luvis weapons was hindered because of the threat of her physical strikes and the fact she could recreate whatever he got rid of with little problem.

In the end, though, this didn't seem to matter to him.

"Enough!"

Andres slammed his fists into the ground, causing a powerful explosion. Daedalus watched as his Luvis shifted in an ominous way that seemed entirely unnatural. It felt insulting for him to watch it. Everything about the way the energy looked to him was a disgusting malformation of what Luvis was in Daedalus's mind.

The effect of the energy matched its appearance. Taking on the form of tendrils, the Luvis whipped forward and ripped at Madam without hesitation. She couldn't see what was happening, how it was destroying huge chunks of her Luvis at a time. It was only when she suddenly stumbled back, appearing lightheaded, that her eyes sparked with realization.

"Madam! Run back!" yelled Daedalus. "He's destroying your Luvis!"

Madam shifted her weak eyes to his from afar. Thankfully, she listened, jumping as far back as she possibly could, her movements shakier than before.

"How do you know that?" growled Andres. His Luvis turned on the shielded group.

"It's a secret," responded Daedalus.

The tendrils swung at Luna's barrier, easily destroying it while phasing through nearly everyone in the group, destroying copious amounts of Luvis. Sending them to the ground. Everyone except Daedalus, who out of instinct tried to block the attack and, somehow, managed to grab hold of the tendril meant to hit him.

"What!?" roared Andres in disbelief.

Daedalus jerked the corrupted Luvis and broke the tendril. He looked first at the floor and then his hands to make sure that had really just happened.

Without thinking much more about it, he ran headfirst toward the opponent that even a Pleiades couldn't defeat.

* * *

Andres was shocked to his core to see his Luvis handled by another Radiant. It bothered him. Angered him. It made him feel filthy knowing that someone had touched his beautiful and prestigious Luvis. All that left him in a frozen state of rage that gave his new opponent enough time to close the distance between them.

He returned to his senses the moment the young man's fist crashed into his face. Without bothering to say anything, the young Radiant unloaded multiple punches against him. They weren't beautiful or clean, or even remotely the moves of someone who had trained to be a fighter. Instead, the attacks were those of a desperate man looking to end it all as fast as possible through brute force, as if he knew that after this one combo, he wouldn't have another chance.

"Gah!"

Blow after blow, punch after punch, the young Radiant let out a war cry right in Andres's face as his fists rapidly descended upon him. Andres couldn't even form a cohesive thought due to the barbaric, savage battering he was receiving.

What made matters worse though, was that the very Luvis that had protected Andres from all of the previous attacks seemed to be ineffective against his new opponent. Rather than stop his attacks, it instead parted ways for his fist and wouldn't make contact with the young man's Luvis.

What the hell! What the hell! What the hell!

Andres's rage was stockpiling with each blow until he finally slammed a foot into the ground. With a roar that shook the whole arena, he unleashed a singular punch that caught the young man's sternum and broke every single bone in his ribcage in multiple places.

"Filthy. Dirty. Pig! You DARE!"

His fist continued forward until it punched a hole right through the man, and his blood splattered for multiple feet behind him along with other bits of his insides. Yet, despite that damage, the young Radiant continued attacking defiantly until Andres pushed in too close to hit. Still, not even that stopped him as he bit down on Andres's neck, intending to rip out his jugular.

"*Animal!*"

* * *

Daedalus focused his Luvis into his teeth as his vision blackened, strengthening them as much as he could. When that didn't work, he focused it solely into his canines. Then, with a rich squish, his teeth dug into his opponent's flesh. Andres's blood filled his mouth.

"Gaaah!!"

It was a desperate hold, and Daedalus did everything he could to keep it. But with his body weakening at a frightening pace, he knew he only had seconds at best to find a way to damage Andres enough to give someone a chance to win the battle.

In response, his opponent ripped his fist out of his chest cavity and tried to push him away, but by now, Daedalus had a deathly grip on him. His eyes were blazing blue with the look of a man who had no fear of death. Not even an ounce of terror was present in Daedalus's eyes. They were filled with a burning desire to win, to overcome. He almost thought he glimpsed a tinge of fear within Andres's face.

Even so, the limitations of the mortal body could only be extended for so long through sheer willpower. Without knowing it, Daedalus passed out while maintaining the exact same pressure.

* * *

Madam watched in alarm as Andres shouted, "Get off!"

He slammed his shoulder down, and Daedalus splatted on the floor with glazed-over but still ferocious-looking eyes.

"Fuck!" yelled Andres, who was holding his neck in an attempt to stop the massive bleeding. "You get to die first!"

A loud, high-pitched shriek rang to life in the distance, and Andres disappeared in a powerful blast of Luvis energy. Madam had prepared an especially large cannon with the time Daedalus bought her, and began firing it without prejudice.

"Gah!"

Each blast threw Andres back a few feet as he attempted to hold his ground, but his own protection against Luvis was starting to falter, and she could tell he was feeling more and more of each blow. When he gritted his teeth as if he had finally regained his defensive capabilities, the slow but deadly barrage intensified.

"Block this," said Madam, coldly.

Without anyone noticing, she had modified her large buster cannon into what could only be called a chain-cannon. It had multiple barrels that were slowly turning to fire at a much faster rate than the single barrel could. And with a snap of Madam's fingers, they rotated at the speed of a normal chain-gun with the rate of fire to match.

Each shot shook the arena violently and made everyone cover their ears. The sound alone was enough to cause significant damage to any person in the vicinity who wasn't properly protected. This included the unconscious Daedalus, but Luna quickly created a barrier around him with a healing field as best as she could from a distance.

Andres looked like he was holding back a yell as he focused all of his strength into defending against the barrage. The force of each round was so powerful that he couldn't destroy it in time, or even if he did, it just allowed two or more other rounds to hit him in the same timeframe. This left him with the only option of turtling up, which was going to wear him out faster than it would Madam.

The battlefield's artificial landscape was destroyed after a few seconds, and only the nearly unbreakable floor was left. Even this started to crack under the force of Madam's attack, until Andres suddenly launched himself backward into the Devil's Breath.

He didn't offer any final words or a one-liner; he simply vanished.

Madam unleashed her gun into the fog, but all the rounds only disappeared into the endless darkness without so much as dispersing the Devil's Breath. What was certain, though, was that Andres wasn't planning on fighting anymore. The wall of poisonous fog rose over the roof, which started crumbling down.

"What to do now?" she muttered.

It was a black sky with no escape, a dome of death, and everyone in the battlefield watched calmly as it descended onto them. At such high concentrations, Madam had no doubt the gas would kill them all. She had no idea how to stop it.

"I can purify this."

Luna dispelled her barrier over Daedalus, but maintained the healing seal. She then quickly drew a long series of runes in the air, and another dome of pink energy expanded outward from her to clash with the gas. A loud hissing filled the air as the two forces met, but not even Luna's purification abilities could overcome the sheer amount of toxin in the air.

"What options do we have?" she asked. Her barrier was shrinking slowly, but still buying them time.

"Gracious death?" suggested Madam. "We could try to make it through, but I doubt we'd make it very far, even at our fastest. Those concentrations are most likely instant death. As I'm sure you all understand."

"If we can punch a large enough hole, perhaps we can make it?" asked another Radiant in the group.

"I'm spent…and Luna is just as tired. Are the rest of you capable of creating enough of a force to punch through a fog even my rounds can't pierce?"

The small group of Radiants all looked at each other. Luna lifted her arms once more to strengthen her barrier, but it proved pointless; the purification field's degradation stayed nearly the same. Only now, she was draining extraordinary amounts of her Luvis to buy everyone time.

"We have to try something!" cried the remaining Electra elder. "Lady Luna is about to give. The time she is buying us is crucial. Once her field falls, it'll only be a matter of seconds!"

"Dragon's Requiem!"

A loud roar ripped through the battlefield. A sound that mimicked the deep, guttural cry of a dragon, but felt oddly melodic in nature. It was a long battle cry, and at first, everyone was confused about what was happening until from the east, the fog began getting blasted away with frightening ease.

The shout lasted for as long as the fog stayed, and even though the voice producing it began to crack, it held until all of the noxious toxin was blown away to the far edges of the arena.

Off in the distance, standing in a new hole on the side of the arena, a battered Alice stumbled forward. Her pink hair hung down in disarray, and her dress was dirtier than it usually was. Even her face looked tired, although that was likely because of the five-foot-seven figure of Frederika slung over her shoulder. She'd somehow recovered her from the arena stands at some point.

"The…show stopper…is here," said Alice, gasping. "Don't worry."

Her voice was raspy and gruff. It showed obvious signs of overuse, and her voice projection was also much grittier than usual. Madam sensed from her wincing that Alice had never experienced torn vocal cords before, and could tell it was something she didn't want to experience again.

"What a sight for sore eyes you are, President," called out Madam.

The fog threatened to crash back onto the battlefield, so without wasting anymore time, everyone hurried to evacuate the area so that they could safely flee. All except for Madam, who spared one more moment to make sure that Andres was truly gone.

Destroying Luvis… she thought as she dematerialized her weapons. *And this young man can see it, too?* Madam turned to look at Daedalus's body, still in an extremely perilous state, in Luna's arms. *There seems to be more at work here than I originally thought... Coincidences like this are often planned.*

CHAPTER 16

Aftermath

"A Radiant who is not only unaffected by Devil's Breath, but can control it and destroy raw Luvis energy? And on top of that *see it*? Are you sure you weren't hallucinating, Madam?"

Susanna Maia threw a leg up onto the large round table in front of her as she leaned back in her chair. Her crimson red hair was styled wildly, and she showed little interest in Madam's report, instead pushing her chair off its front two legs and fidgeting with it.

"It is odd, but not the strangest thing. Is what this Andres does really that different from what we do? We all manipulate Luvis…we just can't do it to other people's Luvis," suggested Eleonora Merope.

"What makes things interesting is that he withstood Madam's barrages. With how much firepower she says she put into it, most of us would have been severely damaged," remarked Tatiana Taygeta. "Aside from

Night, when has there ever been a man as powerful as that? In fact, I don't even think Night could perform such a feat."

Six of the seven Pleiades sat in silence for a moment longer, and Tatiana fixed her short, sleek black hair as part of her bangs fell in front of her eye.

"Any thoughts, Roxy? Svenna?"

Tatiana called out to the two remaining members at the table meant for seven. They both were listening, but one seemed dubious and the other looked mildly amused, as if everything she was hearing was some sort of joke.

"The truth will make itself known. It is not wise to act on incomplete knowledge," said Roxy Celaeno with a sigh, and in response, Svenna Sterope shrugged and let out a chuckle.

"I witnessed this myself. How is that incomplete, Roxy?" demanded Madam, narrowing her eyes.

"Who knows what such a high concentration of Demon's Breath does to Radiants? Perhaps you hallucinated the whole thing. The powers this man possesses are too outlandish even with Eleonora's suggestions. If it were a woman, maybe I'd believe it."

"True, that'd make it more believable," said Eleanora. "Aside from Night, that level of Luvis power is unheard of in males."

"If Night exists, that means there could be more. If we treat him as the exception and not the standard, we risk a lot," argued Madam. "He is an old man. Who knows how many more were born like him within his generation, and how many more after? This Andres character has to be only slightly younger than us."

"You didn't see his face?"

"It was covered by a mask. He also wore a suit and gloves."

"A lot like the old man." Svenna chuckled. "Maybe they are cut from the same cloth."

"Regardless, we should act," stated Tatiana. "What do you think, Susanna?"

"I disagree. Like Roxy said, I need more than just one testimony. I need to see it firsthand."

"Correct," said Roxy. "I need more information before I waste energy like that. Don't you agree, Svenna?"

"Hehe. If it's entertaining, why not let him stir up trouble. It's not like he'll be able to beat us anyways. Perhaps a little mayhem is what we need. Things have been boring lately."

"If you wait to meet him, you might wind up dead…"

"Oy. Watch your tongue, Madam," snapped Susanna, with a threatening look. "We are the Pleiades.

If you want to drum up this guy as a threat to you, do it, but don't put us in the same box."

"I beat you before. If he can withstand me, what makes you think *you'd* win?" growled Madam, her patience waning.

"You'll see once I eventually meet and defeat him."

The strongest Radiants, but that doesn't mean they're the smartest… thought Madam.

"Is that all, then? How are you recovering?" asked Tatiana, clearly wanting to change the subject.

"I took the least damage," said Madam. "The most heavily injured was the Radiant who was invited as a guest by Gold Prominence and the Lightning Empress."

"Oh? They invited the same man? Sounds like a juicy story in the making. Do you think he's dating them together? That would be wild!" Svenna smiled, clapping her hands. "The thought of a night with those two sends a chill up my spine! What a blessed, lucky man."

"He said they were friends. I didn't dig any deeper. I'm not interested in the relationships between Radiants."

"Boo…"

"And you say his actions saved you?" asked Tatiana.

"Yes. They were reckless, inelegant, ugly, and messy, but he went up against an opponent with limited time, so he did as much damage as he could in what little time he had, and it nearly cost him his life. It was brilliant, to say the least, and a good show of his resolve. To make the choice to create as much time as he could and use his own life as a trade…few would do such a thing."

"Resolve? You could call it courage or bravery, I suppose, but it could also be foolishness."

"Perhaps," said Madam. "But I saw his eyes. He knew what he was doing. His actions shifted the outcome of that battle. He also was able to see Andres's attacks. That too saved us all."

"The…Luvis-destroying one?" asked Eleonora as she made a squiggle with her finger to portray the attack.

"Yes."

All the Pleiades looked at each other before wandering off into their own thoughts. Madam eyed them all in turn. It was obvious to her that most didn't have much faith in her word, for no other reason than the fact that she wasn't part of the Seven Great Families. They often gave Night the same treatment, but as the undisputed Seven Star Ruler, it was rarely as effective as it was against Madam. Only Tatiana seemed to want to foster good relations between them and the others, although Night and Madam's mysterious, secretive natures didn't help the cause.

"I suppose that concludes the meeting then. We will all keep an eye out for this Andres character," declared

Tatiana, after a few minutes of silence and obvious intention from everyone present to end the discussion for now.

The Pleiades all shrugged, nodded, or gave other indications that they had heard her, but their interest varied greatly from person to person. Most gave each other quick looks with a certain mockery being felt between their gazes that was aimed at Madam.

"If you need help, Madam, let me know," whispered Tatiana as she stood up to leave.

"It is reassuring to know that at least the Taygeta have a sense of urgency left," said Madam, her cheeks pinched in frustration.

"Now, now, we are all skeptics of different backgrounds. If push comes to shove, I'm sure things will work out. Although, I can't say much about the destruction that will take place before that happens."

Madam shook her head and stood up from her seat. She had given her message and warning, shared the information she needed to and explained everything as best as she could. If they didn't act, then it would only be due to their own hubris. It would be their fault if things worsened. A fine outcome for Madam, who was willing to accept that the Pleiades' lack of action would simply cause destruction, as it usually did.

Still, that didn't mean she was going to remain inactive with them.

* * *

The aftermath of Andres's attack during the Grand Slam left countless people wounded, injured, and in extremely perilous states. All hospitals in the area were soon filled to capacity, but perhaps due to the innate resilience of Radiants, there were no casualties. Regardless, the event was met with scrutiny and heavy criticism from multiple news outlets, and public opinion of Radiants went down significantly, along with the credibility of the universities. Their inability to protect the venue was the main topic of discussion for quite some time.

This was met with forceful retaliation from the three presidents of the universities, whose harsh words toward the reporters and public quickly silenced any dissonance and controversy. They shamed the reporters for taking such a stance during a time of grieving. Alice Alcyone, especially, was harsh as she called them out for attempting to push their anti-Radiant agenda during a time when unity and cooperation was needed. This was only strengthened when Madam herself spoke on the topic and lamented her inability to stop the chaos.

This brought a whole new level of seriousness to the situation, as people began to fear this new threat. Because if not even a Pleiades could stop them, then who could? Still, no one dared to speak ill of the Pleiades like they did the universities, because the power of one of those seven was fear-inducing to the point of inaction.

* * *

"Hm. And here I thought I'd be cheese for the rest of my life."

A few days after the attack, Daedalus woke up in a hospital with blurry vision and moderate shock at the fact that he hadn't died from being turned into Swiss cheese. After a few seconds of consciousness, his mind shifted to a more pressing mystery facing him.

The mystery of why Freya was sitting next to the bed and sleeping with her face in the covers.

"So, you're awake."

Daedalus looked up from Freya and saw Iris standing over him on his left. She looked like death, with heavy bags under her eyes, as if she hadn't slept in days. Despite that, she still had the same intense, regal, and powerful air about her.

"Are...you all right?" asked Daedalus. "You look like hell. Have you been sleeping?"

"You wake up after being unconscious for three days, and the first thing you do is insult my appearance? The audacity," she said, wearing an exhausted smile. "To answer your question, though, I may or may not have been keeping an eye on you this whole time. Well, *we* were, up until a few hours ago when she finally caved."

There was a glimmer of pride in Iris's eye as she swayed gently from side to side.

"You really need to rest."

"Very well."

Iris stumbled forward slightly and crawled into the bed with Daedalus. He furrowed his brow as she wiggled up next to him, and, with a sigh, he both realized and accepted what Iris was doing. When she wrapped her arms around him, he simply started waiting…or at least, he would have if his shoulder weren't wedged into her bosom.

I'm way too tired to think about this, he thought. *Reason, common sense, takes too much energy right now. I'll just go with it…I'm tired…*

Daedalus yawned loudly as his eyes fluttered once again, and Iris echoed him before snuggling closer to his side. At the same time, Freya stirred gently but didn't wake up.

I must have...really worried them...but I guess since I'm here...everything worked out in the end.

He took a moment to look over the two of them and was relieved to see that they were both okay. Within a few more seconds, his eyes slowly drifted closed until he was asleep again.

"Mmm! Mmmm! Mmm!"

After what felt like a second, Daedalus woke up to the sound of muffled complaining. He looked to his left. Iris was clinging desperately to the side of his bed, trying to fight the pull of an irritated-looking Freya, who was covering her mouth and trying to drag her off the bed by her waist.

"Let go," whispered Freya.

"Mmmm!!"

Iris seemed determined to stay in her spot to the point that her efforts to cling to the bed, and Freya's pulling, made the bolted-down legs start to bend, despite the fact neither of them were using their Luvis.

"What...are you doing..."

Freya and Iris both noticed Daedalus was awake at the same time. They both let go of the things they were holding on to in the blink of an eye. This caused Iris to fall onto the floor with a hard thud. She squeaked out an "ow" and then frowned.

"That was my hip!" she complained, jumping back up to her feet. "My hips are one of my most attractive features! What if you bruised it?"

"I didn't realize the Lightning Empress was so fragile that a mere floor could hurt her," replied Freya.

"I'm not using my Luvis! Of course, being dropped on my hip is going to hurt!"

Iris stomped her foot before pausing and clearing her throat to look back at Daedalus.

"Sorry about that. How are you feeling?"

"Good… How was your nap?"

"Heavenly." Iris smiled. "It's amazing how rejuvenating even a bit of sleep can be when in the right environment."

"You mean while being glued to Daedalus?" said Freya.

"Don't be jealous, just because you didn't take the initiative."

"Initiative?" Freya snorted. "You just took advantage of the fact I fell asleep."

"That isn't really my problem, now is it, Stryker?"

Iris cocked her head upward. There seemed to be something different about the two women in front of Daedalus, and part of him felt like he was in danger as they continued arguing amongst themselves. Their words aside, their body language showed that they were both subtly trying to jockey for the closest position to him. Before he could comment on it, Iris flung a finger into his face, cutting off his thoughts.

"My mother told me what happened. She told me the tale of your bravery," Iris said, while still maintaining eye contact with Freya. "You recklessly charged an incredibly dangerous opponent and nearly got yourself killed. Yet, those actions snatched victory out of the enemy's hands and placed it in yours."

"Uh…I wouldn't say I was victorious. I got a big hole in me, didn't I? Which I'm glad isn't still there," corrected Daedalus. He patted his stomach as if he wasn't convinced that he had truly healed.

"You all share in the victory. Your actions gave Madam the opening she needed. Regardless, because of your display, despite your 'weakness' as a Radiant, my mother has decided that she wants you to become a part of the Electra family."

"Huh?"

"After watching you, she has realized that what the Electra lack is a backbone. A spine. An unwavering will and determination. All traits that you exemplify to the extreme. Thus, she would like you to be part of creating the next generation of Electra."

"What are you saying, Electra?" cut in Freya.

She tried to position herself between Daedalus and Iris, as if sensing a threat, but Iris wasn't about to give up being in the middle.

"What I'm saying is that I will be entering a relationship with this man."

"What?!" cried out Freya and Daedalus simultaneously.

"Do you object?"

"Wh—" started Daedalus.

"Yes!" Freya jumped right in. "Daedalus has no reason to enter a relationship with you. Simply because it's convenient for your family? I don't think so. He would much rather...he wou—he..." Her face turned uncharacteristically red. "He would rather be with me! Right?"

Daedalus took a deep breath and put prayer hands up to his lips. He opened his mouth. Closed it. Opened it again with another deep breath, then exhaled again. His brain just wasn't currently capable of processing what was happening, and he couldn't find any words.

"There is more benefit to being with an Electra," said Iris. "Not just socially, but functionally as well. Our family's contributions around the world are well rewarded, and he would never have to worry about anything ever again. Not to mention, I am just as attractive if not more attractive than you are."

"He's living with me," snapped Freya. "It's only natural that if he chooses to have an—an—an advanced relationship with a woman, it would be with me."

"Hardly a valid argument. He can move to my dorm or even the Electra estate."

"I think it's a very valid argument."

Freya marched up to Iris until their bodies pressed into each other. Her hair began glowing gold as she gave Iris an irritated look and Iris returned the gaze as electricity cracked to life around her.

A loud thud echoed throughout the room, and the trio all turned to a nearby wall.

"Oy. I'm trying to sleep!"

From around the corner, a mummy limped out toward the group. Completely covered in bandages from head to toe. It took Freya and Iris a minute to notice the tufts of lavender hair poking out from under the wrappings.

"Instructor Espada? Are you okay?"

"No, I'm not okay! I got burned to a crisp by that damn Devil's Breath, and that damn Luna didn't heal me. So, now I'm stuck like this for who knows how long. Everything itches and I can barely move!"

Frederika turned slowly before sliding back to the other side of the wall. It was a strange sight to see, but it

seemed to sober Freya and Iris a bit. It helped put into perspective just what kind of enemy everyone had fought. If someone as powerful as Frederika had been reduced to such a sorry state, then it was even more impressive that Daedalus had not only survived but been labeled the "hero" of the event.

"Perhaps we can reach a compromise," suggested Iris.

"Compromise, how?" asked Freya.

Daedalus wanted to voice how his own opinion hadn't been taken into account yet, as the two kept discussing amongst themselves, but part of him knew that if he did, he might end up in hot water. Knowing both of their personalities and how unusually heated they both had gotten over the topic, he figured it'd be best to just let them talk it out. Although, the fact that they were both interested in him romantically made Daedalus feel somewhat good about himself.

"How about half-sies? We rotate every other day, like a trial period. Whichever one of us he likes best after a certain amount of time will get to keep him."

"Hm…if he earns the 'right' though…"

"What are the odds of that happening…?"

The openness of being in a polyamorous relationship stemmed from the commonly accepted idea that powerful Radiants had the right to produce as many descendants as they wished with as many people as they wanted. Although, that "right" had to be granted through the approval of either the government, the Pleiades, or the Seven Great Families. Otherwise, the relationship wouldn't be "official" or sanctioned, and it would be subject to much scrutiny, legal troubles, and even fines.

The main reason for this was to help "elevate" the next generation of Radiants, while also removing the "less worthy" in a more humane manner. The logic was that if a powerful Radiant had more children, then their genetics would spread out and have a higher chance of mixing with other powerful Radiants. Ultimately creating stronger Radiants in the following generations.

The rule usually only applied to woman, though. This was because they were the only ones who'd ever reached a strength high enough to earn said approval. In fact, the number of men who had been granted the privilege currently amounted to one person. And this one person was the current Seven Star Ruler, known as "Night."

There had been a lot of talk regarding his personal life and marital affairs, but the sixty-year-old man never spoke about any of it. He often masterfully deflected those sorts of questions and, like Madam, kept much of his life a secret.

"I said can it!" Frederika's voice roared over the wall.

This time, the conversation ceased, but for some reason, it ended with both Freya and Iris shaking hands over some unknown agreement. At the same time, a new yelp echoed throughout the ward, along with a *sploosh* and the rattle of a bucket dancing across the floor.

"Great…" Frederika groaned.

"I'm sorry, I'm sorry, I'm sorry!"

The trio looked at each other, and then Iris cleared her throat and placed her hands on her hips.

"So, the nurse said that once you were awake, to tell her, and then after a few tests, you'd be ready to head out," she said.

"Oh… How do I call the nurse?"

Freya pressed a button on the side of Daedalus's bed, and the trio waited for the nurse to arrive. Once she did, the tests she performed were so simple and quick that Daedalus was able to complete them within minutes. This was a relief to everyone involved, as they all just wanted to go home and unwind. Especially Daedalus.

As soon as he was cleared to go, they all headed home, with Iris yielding to Freya for the day after failing to force herself into the dorm for "at least a few days."

CHAPTER 17

Motivations

Loud thudding noises echoed out as Freya attacked the punching bag in front of her. Each punch was strong enough to destroy any normal bag, but due to the hyper-resistant material and extraordinary weight of the ones used by Regulus, even with Freya's absurd base strength, they bobbed back normally.

Her fists were uncovered, but despite that, her knuckles didn't redden much at all as she continued mindlessly assaulting the bag. Her body was running on autopilot as her mind thought about something else. Namely, the fact that she had prematurely confessed to Daedalus only days ago.

Thinking back, she realized that while she might have suggested entering a relationship with Daedalus, she didn't even know if she had those kinds of feelings toward him. What she did know was that the idea of Iris taking him from her greatly bothered her. That was what had spurred her into action.

Whether that meant she was in love with him, she didn't know. Then again, from what she had read online, it was almost certain that she was. Yet, Freya's idea of "love" wasn't lining up with what she was currently feeling. It was a strange contrast, and as she continued thinking about it, she began to reason that this was because of her own personal inexperience with romance.

Thwack.

Thwack.

Thwack.

The inability to figure herself out was frustrating for Freya. She started using more and more of her power, until the punching bag was flying backward at each hit. When she realized what she was doing, she stopped and took a deep breath to recollect her thoughts.

Romance. Love? I don't even bother thinking about things like that. I came to Regulus to learn how to control my powers, but Daedalus showed me how to finally defeat this curse... With his help, it even became my strongest tool.

Freya threw another punch at the bag.

For what, though? I never cared about being the strongest.

She thought back to the day when Daedalus had found out he hadn't made it into the school. The time they both were in the orientation tournament together. It had been extremely heartbreaking for her, at the time. She had finally made a friend. A real friend, and after getting to know each other, laugh, and train, he was going to leave her forever. Or, so she had originally thought.

"I want you to try your best to become the greatest Radiant ever." Daedalus's words from that day echoed in her mind.

That's right…he gave me a new goal that day. To keep going until he came back again. He told me not to slow down. At the time, I guess I implied I wanted to be the strongest, but I never really cared until he said that as long as I tried my best, he'd be back.

Freya rolled her eyes, realizing just how silly everything was. Yet, at the same time, she was sitting on two championship titles due to that very silliness. A promise that had nothing but her trust in him to back it up. She could have tried her best every year, and Daedalus might have never showed up, but she would have continued just so that at the very least, she could say she upheld her end of the promise. Now, the deal was complete, which left her in another awkward place.

How do I feel about him? And what are my goals now…what's my motivation? To be the best "just because" feels empty…

Freya let out a long sigh and took a few steps back from the punching bag before letting loose a half-hearted kick. The attack was so weak that it didn't even create a notable sound on contact, and as she brought her leg down, she could feel herself losing motivation.

"Hey! What was that?"

From the other punching bag area, Daedalus popped his head over and frowned. Sweat was pouring off his face.

"Are you tired? What's wrong? I've never heard such a wimpy attack come out of you before."

"It's nothing."

"Uh huh, sure. You have the same look you always get when something is bothering you. It happened when you were bothered by your Luvis aura, and I saw it not too long ago when you had to do the photoshoot."

Freya's cheeks warmed as she thought about how well Daedalus knew her. It also put her in an arguably bad position, because that meant she was like an open book to him, despite the fact she was so unexpressive and neutral all the time.

"Why do you fight?" she abruptly asked.

"Huh? Me? Hm, well, I guess at first, I wanted to become a powerful Radiant to spread the word of Striking Tiger Palm in honor of my mother."

"But you don't really use it anymore. You made your own form."

"That's right. Because I saw that it was in good hands with you." He smiled. "I had some trouble accepting that, but when I look at you, it's hard to realistically believe I could overcome such a tall mountain from where I was. That's why I devised a modified form that suited my needs better…and after about a year, I decided that my goal wouldn't be about the form anymore."

"What is it now?"

He shrugged. "It's nothing special. I just want to make my mom proud, live up to the legacy she left behind. I tried thinking of a lot of grand, universal reasons as to why I would try so hard. Save the world, make changes here and there, prove myself…but none of them resonated with me. In the end, the goal that I felt most attuned to was the desire to make my mom in the big sky above smile. So that one day, when my time is up, I can see her again in the great beyond and ask her, 'Hey, did I do good?' and she'll say, 'You did fantastic, son.'"

Daedalus looked up fondly as he took a deep breath.

"Like I said, it's pretty simple. It's not that ambitious. Some people might call it stupid…but, you know, who doesn't want to make their mom proud?

Most people get to hear it off the bat. I have to wait until the end of my life to hear her say it... So, if I have to wait, I'd like to at least give her a nice list to go through, you know? And the first dot on the list is to become one hell of a powerful Radiant."

He sniffed as tears gathered in his eyes. With a sharp cough, he wiped away the liquid and cleared his throat.

"Why do you ask?"

"No rea—"

Freya stopped midsentence. She wanted to say that she'd asked simply out of curiosity, but part of her also wanted to come clean. Daedalus was someone she trusted, and he had helped her with so many different things. There was no reason why this problem would be any different. Even if she was fighting against her innate nature by doing so, eventually her bond with Daedalus prevailed, and she looked at him directly in the eyes to say what was on her mind.

"I ask...because I have no more motivation."

"Oh."

"Yeah."

He was silent for a moment. "Well...I guess we'll just have to go find some, eh?"

"What do you mean?"

"Motivation! It's like most things in this world. You find it, you lose it, sometimes you even misplace it! Crazy stuff, motivation. The trick is just to keep an eye out. It could be that you haven't found that thing to drive you. Or, maybe your motivation lies in something else entirely! Just because you are a gifted Radiant blessed with immense combat skills doesn't mean you have to make it your life. Perhaps there is something else out there that will make you happier."

Happy?

Freya repeated the word in her head. The last time she had felt joy battling someone was when Daedalus stood in front of her for the first time. It was the first time someone of her own age had stood their ground against her, and that battle had made her feel like she was soaring on clouds. After that, the sensation faded as she encountered more opponents who could resist her aura, and since then, the same joy had never resurfaced. She'd just ended up doing what she was doing to uphold her promise with Daedalus.

"What do you think I should do?" she asked.

"That's not really something I can answer for you, Freya. Although, I can definitely help you find an answer. Do some soul searching and exploring. It can be pretty fun."

"What do you think about…being with me?"

Freya took the opportunity as the conversation became more intimate.

"Oh…well." Daedalus scratched his head. "Honestly, I haven't given it much thought. I'm not very experienced in romance, so all of this is pretty new to me. But…I don't know, if it's okay with you, I'd be okay with getting to know you better with…that sort of stuff in mind."

"And things would still be the same? We'd still be friends?"

"Of course. I'd like to think we are friends first before anything else. Sure, a lot of people say it can't be done, and once it fails it all goes south, but we both know that neither of us are very good at fitting into any molds." Daedalus chuckled.

Freya brought her fists up and looked over her knuckles. She had spent her life training to control her Luvis so she would stop being feared. Daedalus had never feared her, and then he'd helped her overcome a lifelong issue while presenting a new temporary goal. Now, her new goal was to find new motivation, but as she continued thinking, part of Freya wanted to believe that maybe her next goal would be to win Daedalus over. As simple as that was.

"I don't think you've talked much about your mom before," commented Freya.

"Yeah, I try not to bring her up too much. Being a 'momma's boy' tends to turn people off. I learned that pretty quick."

"It's not because it's a sensitive issue?"

"Nah, I've come to terms with what happened. That's why I can be who I am. People wouldn't understand because they probably still have their mother, or maybe they just don't like their mom. But...me and my mother had a great relationship, and it probably would have gotten better. We just didn't get much time."

Daedalus closed his eyes as tears once again welled up in his eyes. "I don't know why I always cry when I talk about her," he added with a chuckle. "I really am at peace with what happened. Anyway, that's why I wanted to honor her in some way, and now, I just want to make her proud. Act how she taught me, aspire for greatness and whatnot. I could say I want to be the *best*, but it's not really my main fuel, you know?"

"And your dad?"

"He couldn't handle my mother's death. He used to be a vibrant man. Now he just works and works. We don't talk much. He's still supportive, though, and he's there when I need him, but he's more like a shadow of who he once was. Of course, you know, still better than him being dead."

"Mhm."

An awkward silence spread between the two as the conversation reached its natural end. The two looked around uncertainly, until Daedalus once again cleared his throat.

"I think that's enough melodramatic stuff on my end." He chuckled. "Let's focus for now on finding your new motivation! I'm thinking that maybe step one is a bit of fisticuffs action. So, with that in mind, want to spar? Maybe that will light a few bulbs up."

"Okay."

Freya hopped over the wall around her space and followed him toward the sparring rooms. Even if she was unsure now, she felt that it was okay as long as Daedalus was there, because for some reason, his words and his presence made things feel less confusing.

* * *

"It's cute, isn't?" said a man with a chuckle. "His whole 'I want to make mom proud' spiel. Oh, if only he knew. Isn't that right, 'Mom'?"

Two hooded figures stood on the top of a large building far in the distance, just outside the boundary field that protected the university and alerted the school of unauthorized visitors. One was a large, gruff man whose height dwarfed the other figure's more petite, lithe build.

A pair of cold, emotionless eyes locked onto the laughing man, a certain frigidness in their gaze that would have intimidated almost anyone. Their source was a woman in her early thirties. Her long black hair was tied neatly into a ponytail. She showed no emotion on her face, but her stare alone communicated everything that was necessary.

"Why are we here?" she asked.

"Well, Andres wanted me to keep tabs on him in case he survived. Never expected him to be related to a member of the organization, though. Wants to make 'Mom' proud. What a childish baby. If only he knew the truth, eh, Emilia?"

Emilia looked through the windows of the Regulus University gym at Daedalus. Her eyes closely looked over his body for a few moments, studying him. He looked much different than he had so many years ago. He seemed stronger, and Emilia found herself staring at him longer than she normally would. Her eyes didn't want to look away.

"He doesn't need to be a part of this."

"Oh, but he is. The fact Andres wants him dead already puts him well beyond the point of no return. He doesn't know what he did, and it's his own fault for acting recklessly. Now, he must pay the price. Or do you disagree?"

"Wasting time on a Radiant with such weak strength is a disgusting oversight and misuse of our limited resources. He is no threat to us, and he's not related to our targets—the Pleiades and the Seven Houses."

"Are you sure you aren't just trying to protect your son?"

"Andres is letting his pride get the better of him. We should be observing Madam or those two girls. They seem like real threats. Especially the gold-haired one. Apparently, she showed immunity to the Devil's Breath."

"That a fact? Now, that's interesting. Off topic...but knowing you, you'll keep dodging my question until the world ends. So, I'll let it rest for now. Although, I am curious; I wonder if Andres knew about you two and did this on purpose. It's definitely his type of twisted humor."

"It hardly matters."

"Yeah, I suppose so." The man's gaze shifted back to Daedalus. "I'd kill him now, but without Devil's Breath, it'll probably be difficult. I definitely wouldn't be able to do it before security appeared. Especially now that it's a lot tighter."

"Let's go then. I know you like slacking off and wasting time, but we need to be more productive for the sake of the cause."

"All right, all right, fine. We got enough information to keep Andres off our back as it is. As much as I enjoy seeing the ever-stoic Emilia squirm, I also do believe this is a waste of my time and talents. So, for now, I will yield."

The man took out a small device, and with a click of a button, the two were turned into an array of light particles that zoomed away straight into the sky.

To most people, this went completely undetected, but Freya sensed the sudden shift in Luvis. She looked up to see the last moments of what she thought was a stray star in the sky.

* * *

"It is fortunate that everyone was properly evacuated, my daughter."

"Thank you, Mother."

Luna Electra sat in a large, ornately decorated chair as Iris waited on one knee while looking down. She had just finished giving the head of the Electra family a brief rundown of the events that had taken place during the attack. This included the rapid evacuation of the patrons following the gas, and how she, along with the other competitors, had been ushered to a safe room for the duration of the event.

"It's good that they have emergency bunkers that have filters for Devil's Breath. The RAL has done well," said Luna.

"I believe they deserve praise. The only point of criticism I can make is that they didn't have a space where the civilians in the audience could share in our safety."

"It would be dangerous and nearly impossible to create an extra space that large with the same functionality. It makes sense that competitors who are underground waiting would need a special bunker, as they cannot escape threats from there. They are trapped, after all."

"Of course, Mother."

Iris bowed her head deeper. The doors behind them swung open, and a group of four elderly woman walked in. Two of which were present at the Grand Slam and had fully recovered from Andres's assault.

"Lady Luna, the elders have come to a consensus."

"On what?"

"On the subject of the young Iris's spouse."

Iris gave the elders a sharp look. She hated how the "council" always tried to pair her with people. Usually, this just meant she would have to argue her way out. But this time, she felt it would be easier to "respectfully" turn down their recommendation due to her mother approving of Daedalus in private.

"I have reached my own conclusion on that matter," started Luna.

"I am sure, Lady Luna, but allow us decrepit elders to share some of our wisdom, regardless. It is why we are here, after all. To offer our experience and insight to help the Electra family."

Because that's worked so well... thought Iris, fighting back an eye roll.

"Very well."

The elders walked in front of Iris and bowed lightly while obstructing Iris's view of her mother. A commonplace occurrence that they did simply out of spite and distaste for the young Radiant. It was extremely disrespectful, but at the same time, from the family's standpoint, Iris had no claim to respect or consideration.

"The young Iris has proven to be powerful, but a desecrator of our old ways," began one of the elders. "Her thinking, mannerisms, and actions in the past all have brought nothing but dishonor to our family. This includes the grand insult of losing to a no-name Radiant, Gold Prominence."

"We are aware of Iris's performance and actions thus far, Elder Luiza," stated Luna sharply.

"Of course, I apologize. I understand these truths sour your mouth, but I felt it important to keep them in mind."

The other elders nodded in agreement.

"Back to the matter at hand. Elder Saya and I have come to an agreement over a certain individual, one we encountered recently."

"Who?"

"He is a nobody who was present in the skybox during the Grand Slam. He is of negligible power, but displayed something that we feel would prove useful to the Electra family in future generations."

"You are referring to the Hero of the Assault, correct? Daedalus Notos."

"Yes, Lady Luna. He showed a mental strength that isn't commonly observed in males. A tenacity and determination that isn't normal. We believe that if this is mixed with the young Iris's own strength, the resulting Radiant could very well be extraordinarily powerful. Perhaps even a future Seven Star Ruler."

Luna raised an eyebrow. "Personality traits aren't something that are inherited."

"Correct, Lady Luna, but children learn from their parents. If he is a father to a child who takes after him, then we would achieve the results we are aiming for. Not to mention, his ability to handle an otherwise invisible force—the one that destroyed our Luvis energy in its base form—shows that he hides a powerful ability that we would also greatly benefit from."

"I see. So, you would recommend that Iris put her utmost effort into seducing and creating children with this individual? What of her desire to become an accomplished Radiant?"

"In our humble opinion, Iris's potential to become a noteworthy Radiant has reached its limit. Her positioning in the RAL is notable, but without a single championship title, we unfortunately believe she will not go far in the Professional League. Thus, it would be best to focus on producing the next generation of Radiants, so that she may fulfill her duty to the Electra in some way, at least."

Elder Luiza glanced back at Iris with a condescending look in her eye.

"Perhaps even her child would grant her the honor and glory she lacks."

Iris gripped her knee tightly, but without saying a word, she held her position and waited for Luna to speak. Years of this disrespect had taught Iris how futile it was to try and argue with the elders. They were stubborn, cruel, and short-sighted. Hence why they had come to blows in the past.

"Since when have we become so desperate as to try to assimilate all 'interesting' Radiants?" asked Luna.

"It is what has always been done. In this case, though, if we do not act quickly, the other Seven Families might hear as well and try to take him from our grasp. Of course, we do have an advantage with Iris. All things considered, her physical attractiveness is certainly second to none. A blessing she gained from you, Lady Luna. She can finally be of some use to the Electra in this way."

"So, you are suggesting I seduce this man, even though I might not be interested in him in any way?" Iris cut in.

"Interest and romance have rarely played a part in these kinds of arrangements. Even the esteemed Lady Luna followed her duty and had you. The results, as we can see, were phenomenal in terms of strength, but your personality leaves much to be desired. This new addition may fix that issue."

"I see." Iris lifted her chin. "Very well. Then I will do my best to uphold my duty as an Electra."

The four elders stood frozen in shock at how unusually cooperative Iris was being. They all turned at the same time to face her and were at a loss for words until Luiza cleared her throat.

"In the past, you would vehemently oppose these sorts of suggestions. Has something occurred to make you so cooperative? What could have created such a change of heart after years of audacity?"

Iris shrugged. "I have simply realized that it is time to accept my role and bring some semblance of benefit to the Electra. The events at the Grand Slam have opened my eyes."

"Hm. Perhaps Andres's actions weren't as horrific as I originally thought. It seems they have jarred this girl out of her stupor and into a state of reasonability. Regardless, that is our thoughts, Lady Luna."

A small smile crept onto Luna's lips as she chanced a look at Iris, who was also trying to hold back a laugh. The situation had somehow played out to Iris's favor. Normally, to try and be together with a Radiant of no prestige would result in banishment from the Electra family. But now that the elders had brought forth the idea, it could all proceed smoothly without hindrance. In fact, it would be accurate to say that for the first time, Luna would be able to support her daughter with every power allowed to her as the family head.

Not to mention, this would also placate the elders, who always liked to make sure things went how they wanted. It always had to be *their* idea.

"Is that all then, Elders?"

"Yes, Lady Luna."

"Very well. Then, with this information presented to me, as head of the Electra family, I order Iris Electra to do her best in bringing Daedalus Notos to our family. You will use every talent, skill, and method at your disposal to accomplish this goal—but not anything that would besmirch our family name and bring us dishonor. For the glory of the Electra."

"For the glory of the Electra," echoed everyone else.

Iris stood up and left, reveling in her minor victory. Her worst fear about her interest in Daedalus had been the backlash from the elders, but now, they were unwittingly on her side. To make it even better, they thought that *she* was the one confirming to *their* demands.

With more enthusiasm in her step, Iris left to go carefully coordinate her wardrobe for the days when she would and wouldn't see Daedalus, while taking into account the odds of accidentally seeing him on certain days. All with the grand goal in mind of sweeping him off his feet.

EPILOGUE

Brightest Night

The reek of blood and a crimson mist wafted through the air. Inside a large room, a singular man sat in an unassuming fold-up chair. His crimson eyes glowed in the pitch blackness of the room, and not even the soft moonlight passing through the remarkably pristine windows could pierce the darkness inside the space.

His suit was clean and pressed, devoid of any creases or specks of blood, but all around him, the corpses of countless individuals lay strewn across the floor. Their bodies seeped more and more blood onto the once pristine hardwood planks.

"Do you suppose this is due to him?" asked a disembodied woman's voice.

"Without a doubt."

"Should I go see if I can find any other surprises?"

"I have my shade on it."

The woman's voice let out a soft "hm." Then, in a flash of light, the silhouette of a young woman began taking form as white Luvis energy accumulated into one place. Eventually, the silhouette gained features and dimensionality, until a woman of medium height stood in the middle of the room.

"This is disgusting." She chuckled, lifting her bare feet up.

The woman had no clothes on, but at the same time, she lacked the very things that most people would say needed to be covered up. Which made her feel like she wasn't a human, but rather something taking on the human form. With the proper clothing, though, it would be impossible to tell, as her eyes held an authentic vibrancy that many people lacked.

"I've told you to materialize with clothing," murmured the man in his gravelly voice.

"Right, sorry. I forget."

The woman snapped her fingers, and a flowery dress with a matching straw hat popped into existence upon her body in a sparkly show of mystical white lights. Stylish sandals appeared a moment later to match her outfit, despite the fact that summer was long gone.

"Better?" asked Mina.

"Is this the mythical Mina?"

Another voice joined the duo, and the man lazily brought his gaze over to an open window. A few seconds later, the blood on the floor rippled, and footsteps appeared as a cloaked intruder made their way forward. Neither Mina nor the crimson-eyed man seemed to care much.

"Emilia." The man nodded to the intruder.

"Ray."

"Have you come to collect your comrades?"

"No, I advised against this because I still have the utmost respect for your strength. Unlike Andres, who believes you have grown old and senile. The ones here agreed—volunteered, no less—to do this."

"You look like you haven't aged a day, Emilia. You were only ten years younger than me. Now...it looks more like thirty. Is your humanity also something else you've abandoned for the sake of your goals?"

"Consider it a side effect, Ray."

"I doubt it matters, Emilia. I should've seen the signs when you pushed yourself to the point your health declined. Then, you abandoned your family...and now your humanity. How much more is there to give up for the sake of this 'grand goal'?"

Emilia made a complicated face. It was only in the presence of her old friend that she was willing to break her emotionlessness, and that was because he had seen too many sides of her. Usually, her lack of expressing was helpful, but against Ray, it would probably only be detrimental and give more away than anything else.

"You still don't understand."

"I don't. Which is odd. I have become old, and some might even say wise, yet…I still can't fathom what you are thinking. We share similar ideologies, as well. Many called us two sides of the same coin, but now we stand on opposite sides."

"Out of your own choice!" Emilia snapped, her voice rising. "You always talked about the current system and its flaws. But you never did anything to change it! I. *Me*. I am the one taking the steps to create that change. Not you! You do nothing, and that is what makes us different. Our actions. Although, I'm sure I can convince Andres to allow you to join us, if you want to change that."

"I have no interest in allying with a radical terrorist. His arrogance and audacity will lead to his demise in due time. Long before I die of old age, and let me tell you, old friend, I have grown quite old."

"Yet, due to Mina, you remain as powerful as before."

"It is only because of Mina that I became powerful. But that is neither here nor there. I refuse to stand with you and your dangerous maverick."

"Ironic that you of all people would call someone a maverick."

Ray's brow creased. "I'm not working toward a selfish goal. I have the betterment of the world in my plans, along with her people! This isn't just about myself and some foolish belief that I am owed anything."

"You and Andres are the same. You both are willing to kill. There's no difference between you two. You just try to make yourself sound less heinous because you are just as egotistical."

Emilia stomped her foot against the floor, sending drops of blood into the air. Some were close to hitting Ray's suit, but before they touched the fabric, an arm made of darkness reached out of the floor and blocked them before disappearing back into his shadow.

"If that is what you believe, so be it. You are a stubborn woman, as always... On to a different topic. Did you only come here to see Mina for yourself and confirm if I was subdued by these...lackies?"

"I came to warn an old friend. Although, after today, if we meet again, it will be as enemies, and you will have to die, Ray."

"If you make the choice to fight me, I will do you the great respect of cutting you down as quickly as possible. I may be old, but I do not intend to add a single loss to our record."

The glow in Ray's eyes intensified as a warm smile spread across his lips, and Emilia gained a powerful golden aura around her. But instead of sharing his smile, she had a sad frown on her face, along with a pained look in her iris.

"I'm stronger than I was before."

"No. No, you aren't," corrected Ray, without hesitation. "You gave up on your old life and have thrown everything away for the sake of this goal. It's truly a disappointing turn of events for someone I once proudly called my equal. Hopefully, your son does not follow in your folly."

"What's the point of bringing him up? He will live a normal life, blissfully unaware of all of this. Andres has his eye on him, but if Daedalus continues life as he has, without making a ruckus, then he will be fine. He was blessed to be unlike me or you. He has no great power. No great role."

Ray took a small breath before letting out a short mocking laugh. The sound alone irritated Emilia, who was used to hearing it in situations where Ray often thought himself correct. It was like he was calling her idiotic without saying it, although in the past, he would often follow it with the word "fool."

"Fool."

In the background, Mina conjured up a mop and began cleaning all the blood on the floor while throwing the corpses into some sort of hole created out of Luvis. As she worked, she whistled the tune of, "I've Been Working on the Railroad," and would occasionally drop to her knees to take bits of especially stuck "grime" out of the floorboards.

"Enough of this," snapped Emilia. "I gave you my warning. I will take my leave."

"That is fine with me. I would rather not have my memory of you ruined any further. Although, before you go, I have a question. You abandoned your family, but are you capable of cutting down your own son for the sake of your goals?"

"A stupid question, because it will never come to that. Daedalus and my goals are not intertwined, nor will they cross."

"That doesn't answer my question."

Emilia stepped up to the windowsill and looked back at Ray bitterly before jumping down without another word.

* * *

Ray sighed once she was gone. He knew from that short interaction that at the end of the day, his old friend's plans were going to be thwarted by the very things she'd sacrificed to achieve them. It was a shame that she was so blinded that she couldn't realize it.

"A shame, don't you think?" asked Mina, as she pushed the last body into the Luvis portal.

"It is."

The room now clean, Ray picked up the folded chair and placed it under his arm as his cane rose out from the shadows beneath him. Clicking the floor a few times, Ray then cocked his head as his mood shifted, and he casually took out a small pocket watch from his pocket.

"She should be getting off soon, right?"

"You know, if you visit her so much, she won't have a chance to miss you."

"And why would I want that?"

"Because if she misses you, then she'll be even happier once she sees you!" Mina smiled.

"Hm. That's a fair point. Maybe I should visit every other day?"

"Once a week!"

"O-Once a week!" Ray started coughing violently, and Mina smacked his back until he finally calmed down. "That's too long! I'll die, in that case!"

"Twice a week?"

Ray stumbled in place.

"I guess we can start with every other day," she said.

"Thank you." He sighed.

Ray looked out the window of the now sparkling room and took in the beautiful night sky stretching infinitely across the world. A lot of things needed to be done, and while he thought he had everything figured out, a new piece appeared that Ray felt would prove to be problematic if it fell into the wrong hands.

"You'll kill him, won't you?" asked Mina, floating next to Ray as he made his way to the ground floor.

"Only if he makes the wrong choices."

"What if you can't?"

"Then I was the one who was wrong all along…"

"And if you die to Andres?"

"I won't."

"Why?"

"Because I *know* he's wrong."

www.ingramcontent.com/pod-product-compliance
Lightning Source LLC
Chambersburg PA
CBHW031559240626

47153CB00002B/561